D1084697

Binti:
The Night Masquerade

BOOKS BY NNEDI OKORAFOR

THE BINTI TRILOGY

Binti

Binti: Home

Binti: The Night Masquerade

Remote Control

Who Fears Death

Kabu Kabu

Lagoon

The Book of Phoenix

YOUNGER READERS

Chicken in the Kitchen

Zahrah the Windseeker (as Nnedi Okorafor-Mbachu)

The Shadow Speaker (as Nnedi Okorafor-Mbachu)

Akata Witch

Akata Warrior

The Girl with the Magic Hands

Long Juju Man

NNEDI OKORAFOR

BINTI

THE NIGHT MASQUERADE

A TOM DOHERTY ASSOCIATES BOOK
NEW YORK

This is a work of fiction. All of the characters, organizations, and events portrayed in this novella are either products of the author's imagination or are used fictitiously.

BINTI: THE NIGHT MASQUERADE

Edited by Lee Harris

A Tor.com Book
Published by Tom Doherty Associates
175 Fifth Avenue
New York, NY 10010

www.tor.com

The Library of Congress Cataloging-in-Publication Data is available upon request.

ISBN 978-1-250-20344-1 (hardcover)
ISBN 978-0-7653-9312-8 (ebook)

First Edition: January 2018
First Hardcover Edition: July 2018

0 9 8 7 6 5 4 3 2 1

Dedicated to those who aren't supposed to see
the Night Masquerade, but see it anyway.
May you have the courage to answer
the Call to Adventure.

Binti:
The Night Masquerade

Chapter 1

Aliens

It started with a nightmare . . .

"We still cannot get out," my terrified father told me. His eyes were stunned and twitchy. He was underground. We were in the cellar of the Root, the family home. Everyone was. Covered in dust, coughing from the smoke. But only my father was looking at me. I could hear my little sister Peraa nearby asking in a terrified voice between coughs, "What's wrong with Papa? Why's he doing that with his hands?"

My perspective pulled back and now I was just looking at it happening. My family was trapped in there. My father, two of my uncles, one of my aunts, three of my sisters, two of my brothers. I saw several of my neighbors in there too. Why was everyone in there in the first place? All huddled in the center of the room, grasping each other, wrapping themselves with their veils trying to hide, crying, tears running through otjize, *praying, trying to call for help with their astrolabes. Bunches of water grass, piles of yams, sacks of pumpkin seeds, dried dates, containers of spices sat in corners. Smoke was coming through the fibrous ceiling and walls of the cellar. The old security drone that had stopped working before I was born still sat in the corner covered with its woven mat.*

"Where is Mama?" I asked. Then more demandingly, I said, "Where is MAMA?! I don't see her, Papa."

"But the walls will protect us," my father said.

I felt the pressure of his strong hands as he grasped me. They didn't feel arthritic at all. "The Root is the root," he said. "We will be okay. Stay where you are." He brought his face close to mine, then the words appeared before my eyes. Red as blood. "Because they are looking for you."

"Where is Mama?" I asked again, this time waving my hands in my nightmare, as I clumsily used the zinariya, the activated alien technology in my DNA.

But I was suddenly in the dark, alone with my words, as they floated before me like red desert spirits. Where is Mama? *Instead, the sound of hundreds of Meduse thrumming filled my head and the vibration traveled deep into my flesh. Laughter. Angry laughter. I sensed anticipation, too. "Binti, we will make them pay," a voice rumbled in Meduse. But it wasn't Okwu. Where was Okwu . . . ?*

~

I awoke to the universe. Out here in the desert, the night sky was so bright with stars. It was almost as clear as the sky when I'd been on the Third Fish traveling to and from

Earth. I stared up, hearing, seeing, and balanced equations whispered around me like smoke. I'd been treeing in my sleep. It was that bad. I hadn't even done this while in the Third Fish after the Meduse killed everyone but me. I was having so much trouble adjusting to the zinariya. That wasn't just a dream about my family, it was also a message sent using the zinariya from my father. I couldn't awaken fully before receiving it and so my mind protected me from the stress of it by treeing.

Mwinyi and I had left the village on camelback hours ago and then we'd stopped to rest. I'd lain in the tent Mwinyi set up, while he'd gone off for a walk. I was so exhausted, scared for my family, and overwhelmed. Everything around me felt off. Trying to get some sleep had not been a good idea.

"Home," I whispered, rubbing my face. "Need to get . . ." I stared at the sky. "What is that?"

One of the stars was falling toward me. The zinariya, again. "Please stop," I said. "Enough." But it didn't stop. No. It kept coming. It had more to tell me, whether I was ready or not. Its golden light expanded as it descended and I was so mesmerized by its smooth approach that I didn't tree. When it was mere yards above, it exploded into showers of brilliance. It fell on me like the golden legs of a giant spider and then the zinairya made me remember things that had never happened to me.

~

I remembered when . . .

Kande was washing the dishes. She was exhausted and she had more studying to do, but her younger twin brothers had wanted a late night snack of roasted corn and groundnuts and they'd left their stupid dishes. How they'd managed to eat something so heavy this late at night was beyond her, but she knew her parents wouldn't complain. This was why at the age of six they were so plump. Her parents never complained about her brothers. Still, if Kande left the dishes for the morning, the ants would come. It was a humid night, so she knew other things would come too. She shuddered; Kande detested any type of beetle.

She finished the dishes and looked at the empty sink for a moment. She dried her hands and picked up her mobile phone. It was already eleven o'clock. If she focused, she could get a good hour of studying in and still manage five hours of sleep. In her final year in high school, she was ranked number six in her class. She wasn't sure if this was good enough to be accepted into the University of Ibadan, but she certainly planned to find out.

She put her phone in her skirt pocket and switched off the light. Then she stepped into the hallway and listened for a moment. Her parents were watching TV in their room and the light in her brothers' room was off. Good. She turned and tiptoed to the front of the house, quietly unlocked the door, and sneaked outside. It was a cool night and she could see the open desert just beyond the last few homes in the village.

Kande leaned against the side of the house as she brought out a pack of cigarettes from her skirt pocket. She shook one out, placed it between her lips, and brought out a match. Striking the match with her thumbnail, she used it to light her cigarette. She inhaled the smoke and when she exhaled it, she felt as if all her problems floated away with it—the ugly face of the man her parents said she was now betrothed to, the money she needed to buy her uniform for her school dance group, whether Tanko still loved her now that he knew she was betrothed.

She took another pull from her cigarette and smiled as she exhaled. Her father would be furious and beat her if he knew she had such a filthy habit. Her mother would wail and say no man would want her if she didn't start behaving, that she was too old for rebellion. Kande was looking toward the desert as she thought about all this and when she first saw them, she was sure that her brain was trying to distract her from her own dark thoughts.

They were a house away before she even moved. And by then, she was sure they'd seen her. Tall, like human palm trees and not human at all. And even in the moonlight, she saw that they were gold. Pure shiny gold. Not human at all. But with legs. Arms. Bodies. Long and thin like trees. Walking slowly toward her in the night. There wasn't another soul silly enough to be outside at this time of night. Just her.

Kande didn't know it, but everything depended on those moments after she saw them. What she did. The destiny of her people was in her hands. She stared up at the aliens who saw themselves as one thing but accepted the name of "Zinariya" (which meant "gold") that human beings gave them and . . .

~

. . . I fell out of the tree. Mwinyi was shaking me. Gusts of sand and dust slapped at my skin when I turned to him and I coughed hard.

"Binti! Come on! Pull yourself out of it!"

At first, I saw all things around me as the sums of equations, numbers splitting and unfurling, falling away, rotating, all in harmony. My eyes focused on his tall lanky frame; his caftan and pants that were blue like Okwu flapped in the sandy wind. Grains of sand blew about pretending chaos, but each arced a trajectory that coincided with those around it. I shook my head, trying to come back to myself. My mouth had been hanging open and I spit out sand.

I twitched as a rage flew into me like an explosion. *My family!* I thought, frantic. *My family!* Before I could shout this at Mwinyi . . . I saw Okwu hovering behind him. My eyes widened and my mouth hung open again. Then Okwu was gone. Instead, behind Mwinyi were small skinny red-furred dogs; they ran about flinging their heads this way and that way. I felt one touch my face with its cool black nose, sniffing. It yipped, the sound close to my ear. The dogs were running all around us, at least as far as I could see, which was only a few feet. Our camel Rakumi was roaring with distress. I was seeing words now as Mwinyi desperately tried to reach me using the zinariya.

The floating green words said, "Sandstorm. Dog pack. Relax. Grab Rakumi's saddle, Binti."

I am not a follower, but there are times when all you can do is follow. And so yet again, I submitted. This time it was to Mwinyi, a boy I had only known for a few days, of a people I'd viewed as barbarians all my life and now knew were not, my father's people, my people.

I was breaking and breaking and into that moment I followed Mwinyi. He led us out of that sandstorm.

~

The sun broke through.

The air cleared of dust.

The storm was behind us.

I sighed, relieved. Then the weight of the sudden quiet made my legs buckle and I sank to the ground at the hooves of our camel Rakumi. I pressed my cheek to the sand and was surprised by its warmth. There I lay, staring at the retreating sandstorm. It looked like a large brown beast who'd decided to leave, when really it just happened to travel the other way. Churning, roiling, and swirling back the way we'd come. Toward the Enyi Zinariya village. Away from my dying, maybe even dead, family.

I weakly raised my hands and moved them slowly, typing in the air. The various names of my father. Moaoogo Dambu Kaipka Okechukwu. I tried to send it. But they wouldn't go. I rolled my head to the side in the sand, feeling the grains ground into my *otjize*-rolled *okuoko,* blue tentacles layered with sweet-smelling red clay and now sand. I tried to call Okwu. I tried to reach it. To touch it with my mind as I had days ago, now. Again, nothing.

Then I started weeping, as the world around me began to do that expanding thing that it had been doing since we'd left the Ariya's cavern over a day ago. As if everything were growing bigger and bigger and bigger, though it was still the same. Mwinyi said it was just my body settling with the zinariya technology that Ariya had unlocked within me, but what did that matter? It didn't make it any better. The sensation was so jarring that I constantly felt the Earth would decide to fling me into space at any moment.

I shut my eyes and it was as if I'd fallen again. Into my other nightmare. The nightmare from a year ago. Now I was back on the Third Fish, sitting at the dining hall table. I could taste the sweet milky dessert in my mouth. My *edan* was in my hand, the strange gold ball back inside the stellated cube–shaped metal shell; it was whole again. And I was gazing at Heru, the beautiful boy who'd noticed that I'd braided my *otjize*-rolled locks into a tessellating triangle pattern that reflected my heritage. His granite black hair was falling over one of his eyes as he laughed. He glanced at me, and I smiled. And then his chest burst open and his warm blood spattered on my face and I fled within myself, quivering, silently screaming, breaking. Everyone was dead.

The dining hall grew red, even the air took on a red tint. There was Okwu, behind Heru. I could smell blood, as I tasted the sweet milky dessert in my mouth. Everyone was dead. I had to survive. I slowly got up, clutching the *edan* in my hand, and when I turned, it wasn't a Meduse I faced but my cowering family inside the bowels of the Root. In the large room, below, where all the foodstuffs and supplies were stored.

The smell of blood turned to one of smoke. I'd moved from one nightmare to another. My eye first fell on my oldest sister shrieking in a corner as her long, long hair went up in flames. I was coughing and then looking frantically around as I waited to smell the burning of my own flesh because flames were consuming the entire room. Now my family was all around me, my father, siblings, several of my cousins, aunts, uncles, nieces, nephews, shrieking, stumbling, thrashing, lying still as they burned. Everyone was burning, alive or already dead.

I whimpered, my flesh feeling too hot. *Let me die too,* I thought, waiting, hoping, for the burning to intensify. *My family.* Instead, the fire consuming my family stopped biting me and shrank away. It calmed. It didn't stink of burning flesh now. The fire smelled woodsy and the center of it looked like a pile of glowing rubies. Everything undulated and when it resettled, things looked more real, no red tint, so solid and clear that I could touch the dry ground beneath me, warm my hand at the fire before me.

I distantly felt my *okuoko* writhing with anger. I reached up, grasping them, trying to calm their wriggling. All this was confusing me. I was just coming out of flashbacks of the deaths of my friends and family and now the zinariya was forcing history on me again . . .

~

The old man was named Takeagoodposition. He stood before five other old people, holding a slender pipe to his lips. The smoke smelled sweet and thick and when it blended with the smoke from the fire, it smelled awful.

"The child is a dolt," Takeagoodposition said. "Kande is one of those girls who would follow a lion to her death if the lion flashed a pretty grin."

The men in the group all laughed and nodded.

"No, we won't put the community in the hands of a girl; how would we look?"

"But they came to her first," a tall man said, his long legs crossed before him. "And let's be honest, if those things had come to any of us, what would we have done? Fled? Fainted? Tried to shoot them? But she somehow learned to speak with them, gained their trust. "

"Look what it cost her," the only woman in the group said. "She is like a girl possessed, seeing things that are not there."

"My grandson said it was like they put alien Internet in her brain," another elder said.

There was more soft laughter.

Takeagoodposition frowned deeply. "None of that matters now," he snapped. "The Koran says to be kind and open to strangers. Let us welcome them. The girl will introduce us and we will take over."

"Have you seen them?" another of the men asked. "They're beautiful, especially in the sun."

"And probably worth millions if we divide them into coinage," someone remarked.

Laughter.

"These Zinariya, they are aliens," Takeagoodposition said. "We'll be cautious."

It was as if I were sitting with the men and woman. Listening to them talk about the Zinariya. Some movement behind a cluster of dry bushes caught my eye and I was sure I saw someone slowly back away and then run off.

"Kande," a woman's voice said. It seemed to come from all around me. "She did well, for a child who liked to smoke."

I frowned, wanting to stop all this nonsense and scream, "What does smoking have to do with aliens?!" But then I saw something bouncing around within the circle of people. A giant red ball. It disappeared in the swirls of dust and then bounced back on the ground. It rolled up to me and flattened, shaped like a red candylike button embedded in the sand.

I stared at it.

"Press it." The words appeared in front of me in neat and careful green and then faded like smoke. Mwinyi was speaking to me through the zinariya.

I smashed the button with my fist, vaguely feeling the button's hardness. I heard a soft satisfying click. Everything went quiet. Nothing but the sound of the soft wind rolling across the desert. I rested my forehead on the sand, weeping again.

"Can you get up?" Mwinyi asked, kneeling beside me. "Has it stopped?"

I raised my head and looked up at him. His bushy red-brown hair was coated with sand and the long lock that grew in the back of his head was dragging on the ground beside my knee, collecting more sand. The world behind him, the blue sky, the sun, started expanding again. But not as badly as before, nor was I seeing the death of everything I loved. But I knew of it.

I opened my mouth and screamed, "Everyone's dead!" I rolled to the side, grinding the other side of my head into the sand. My face to the sand, feeling its heat on my skin and blowing out sand, I wailed, "MY FAMILY!!!! I DIE! EVERYTHING IS DEAD! WHY AM I ALIVE?! OOOOOOH!" I sobbed and sobbed, curling in on myself, shutting my eyes. I felt him press a hand to my shoulder.

"Binti," he said. "Your family—"

"DON'T! LEAVE ME ALONE!"

I heard him angrily suck his teeth. Then he must have walked away.

I don't know how long he left me there, but when he pulled me to a sitting position, I was too defeated to fight him. I slumped there, the hot sun beating down on my shoulders.

He sat across from me, looking annoyed.

"I don't have a home anymore," I said. I felt my *okuoko* writhe on my head.

"Ah, there's the Meduse in you," he said.

"I am *Himba,*" I snapped.

"Binti, they might be alive," Mwinyi said. "Your grandmother back in my village communicated with your father in Osemba."

I stared at him, shuddering as I tried to hold back the flash of rage that flew through me. I couldn't and it burst forth like Meduse gas. "I saw them trapped . . . I SAW THEM!" I shouted. "I smelled them b-b-burning!"

"Binti," he said. "Remember, you've just been unlocked! And you have that Meduse blood. I've heard you whimpering in your sleep about what happened last year on that ship. And we're out here in this desert, exhausted and far from your home. You're all mixed up. Some of what you see is communication, some is probably the zinariya showing you stuff it wants you to know, but some is delusion, nightmare."

I raised a hand for him to be quiet and rested my chin to my chest; I was so exhausted now. Tears spilled from my eyes. Everything I'd seen was so real. "I don't know anything," I softly said.

I felt Mwinyi looking at me. "Your father said the Khoush came after Okwu," he said. "They don't know what happened."

"Who is 'they'?" I asked.

"Your grandmother and father. As I'm sure you know, your Okwu is a small army in itself. Your family took shelter in the Root when the fighting began."

"So they *are* in the cellar," I muttered. "That part is true."

"Yes."

I had to process the idea that my father had spoken with my grandmother through the zinariya. "When?" I asked. "When did he talk to her?"

"Just after you were unlocked."

"Just after I sensed Okwu was in trouble," I said. "So he could be—"

"I don't know, Binti. We don't know. Sometimes when the zinariya communicates, it disregards time. We're going to find out."

"You could have told me hours ago."

Mwinyi paused, his lips pursed. "They told me not to. They didn't think the news would help you."

When I said nothing to this, he said, "If you want to get home to help, we can't waste time like this."

I glared at him.

"Don't give me that look," he said. "Aim your Meduse rage that way." He pointed ahead of us. "Last night, I thought I was free to do whatever I wanted. Instead, I'm here, taking you to what can't be a place of peace. And I do care about your family; I'm doing my best."

I ran my hand down my face, wiping away tears, sweat, snot. I paused, realizing I'd probably also just wiped a lot of my *otjize* from my face too. I sighed, flaring my nostrils. Everything was so wrong. "You don't have to take me anyw—"

"I *do* and I will," he said. "You want to know what I think?" He looked at me for a moment, clearly trying to decide if it was better to keep his words to himself.

"Go on," I urged him. "I want to hear this."

"You try too hard to be everything, please everyone. Himba, Meduse, Enyi Zinariya, Khoush ambassador. You can't. You're a harmonizer. We bring peace because we are stable, simple, clear. What have you brought since you came back to Earth, Binti?"

I stared nakedly at him; the hot breeze blowing on my wet face felt cool. My *okuoko* had stopped writhing. I felt deflated. "I need my family," I said hoarsely.

He nodded. "I know."

I grabbed the sides of my orange-red wrapper as I looked straight ahead, toward where we were to go. Right before my eyes, the world seemed to expand, while staying the same, as if reality were breathing. It was a most disconcerting sight. I let myself lightly tree, as I took in several deep breaths. "Everything is . . . still looks as if it's growing," I said. I looked directly at him for the first time. "I . . . I know that sounds crazy, but that's really what I'm *seeing*."

Mwinyi frowned at me, twirling his long matted lock

with his left hand, two of the small brown wild dogs sitting on either side of him like soldiers. Then he said, "I can get you home, but I don't . . . I don't know how to help you, Binti. I never needed to be 'activated'; I don't even know what you're going through."

I clutched the front of my orange-red top and whimpered, thinking of my family back in Osemba. After traveling all day, then through the night, we'd traveled much of the next day. When the sun was at its highest, we'd settled down in our tent for some rest. We'd finally fallen asleep when the sandstorm hit. "I know you think I'm too much but—"

"That's not what I said."

I cut my eyes at him. "You did. Don't worry, it's not the first time something like this has happened to me," I said, shutting my eyes for a moment. When I opened them, I felt a little better. "Let's keep going. We can travel through the night again."

When I tried to get up, he quickly stood and said, "No. Rest."

"I'm okay," I said. "Just give me a minute and we can go as soon as—"

"Binti, we stop. You have to rest. The zinariya is—"

"But if they're in the cellar . . ." I started shaking again. I wrung my hands, my heart beating fast.

"Whatever is happening there, we can't stop it," he said.

I tried to get up and he put a hand firmly on my shoulder. I wanted to fight him, but the feeling of vertigo was back and I could only roll to my side in the dirt, shuddering with misplaced outrage, my *okuoko* writhing again.

"We're making fast time, but we're still a day away," he said. "Binti . . . calm down. Breathe."

"Even with the wild animals out here? The slower we go, the more we risk—"

"Wild animals don't scare me," Mwinyi flatly said, looking me so deeply in the eyes that everything around me dropped away. My *okuoko* slowly settled on my shoulders and down my back. The Meduse rage, which I was still learning to control, left me like cool air flees the morning sun. There is nothing like gazing into the eyes of a harmonizer when you are also a harmonizer.

We stayed and without further exchanging words, we set up camp. I was glad when he walked off into the desert for an hour to see if he could find anything fresh to eat, the small pack of dogs following him like curious children. I needed the quiet. I needed to be alone with . . . it.

"It's not something to learn," he said, over his shoulder. "It's *part* of you now. Intuit it."

And that I understood. I sat on the woven raffia mat in the open tent. I had been studying my *edan* for over a year—a mysterious object I'd found in a mysterious place in the desert, whose purpose I did not know, and whose functions I had first learned of by accident. An object that had saved my life, been the focus of my major at Oomza

Uni, and was now in about thirty tiny triangular metal pieces and a gold ball in my pocket. Yes, I understood intuiting things.

I brought up my hands and used the vague virtual device that rose before me to type out Mwinyi's name and the word "Hello" in Otjihimba. Then I envisioned Mwinyi, who was most likely on the other side of the sand dune he'd disappeared over. Before I saw him in my mind, I felt his nearness, his alertness. He was monitoring me, even from where he was; I wasn't just guessing this, I knew it for a fact. His response appeared before me in green letters that were a different style from mine, neat but relaxed and in Otjihimba, "Are you alright?"

"Yes," I responded.

Then, yet again, I tried to reach my father. "Papa," I wrote. I tried to push the red letters as I held my father's image in my mind. It was as if the words were fixed onto a wall, I couldn't send or even move them. I waved my hands and the words disappeared. I tried another five times before giving up, growing increasingly more agitated, the letters looking sloppier and sloppier. I wiped tears from my cheeks and then before my mind started going dark again, I tried reaching out to Okwu. Five times. Again, nothing.

I rubbed my eyes and when I looked at the backs of my hands, for the first time in hours, I realized that they were nearly free of *otjize*. I gasped, touching my face, looking at my arms, my legs. The sand from the storm had stripped most of it away. Mwinyi had said nothing about this, or maybe he hadn't noticed. I felt like shrieking as I fumbled with my satchel. I had about half a jar left. When I'd arrived on Earth, I'd assumed I would have time to make more.

I gazed at the jar. The red paste wasn't as rich as the one I could make from the clay I dug up around the Root. It was *otjize* different from any *otjize* made by a Himba girl or woman. Mine was from a different planet. I held it to my nose and sniffed its rich scent and saw the tall trees of the forest where I collected the clay, the piglike creature who foraged in the bushes. I saw the face of Professor Okpala, the large pitcher plants that grew beside the station, my classmates, like Haifa and Wan. However, I also saw the Root. And the faces of my family, the dusty roads of Osemba and its tranquil lake.

Rubbing it onto my face, I looked out at the desert. Dry, expansive, free. I inhaled deeply, to control my breathing. No more tears that would wash away the *otjize* I'd just put on my face. And I did what I'd unconsciously done with my *edan* on the Third Fish, but this time instead of speaking to my *edan,* I spoke to the zinariya. And it answered. It was gentle and kind, but I didn't have the unaffected fresh mind of a baby. I was seventeen years old, the second youngest girl in my family, who'd been tapped to be my community's next harmonizer. I'd instead chosen to leave Earth and go to Oomza Uni and nearly died for my choice. I'd lived and then learned, so much. To engage with the zinariya was to overwhelm all my senses. In the distance, I saw a yawning black tunnel swallowing the soft light of the setting sun.

I don't know what happened.

Mwinyi returned an hour later carrying two dead rabbits. He found me lying on the mat, saliva dribbling from the side of my mouth. I'd watched him approach through dry gummy eyes. As I gasped his name and weakly typed it on the virtual device now hovering on my lap, I saw the red word appear before me. His name floated above him, slowly descending onto his head, where it settled and oozed onto him like melted candle wax. I groaned and when I did, I saw the phonetic spelling of the sound creep from my mouth onto the sand like a caterpillar. It was as if the zinariya itself was mocking me.

It was all too much and when I tried treeing to make it better, my world filled with so many numbers that I felt as if I'd kicked a hornet's nest. I couldn't see around me and some of the numbers grew more aggressive the angrier I got, zooming around and darting at me.

"How am I supposed to get up tomorrow?" I whispered. "So I can . . . my family." I started weeping, though I knew it would wash off even more of my *otjize*. I turned away from Mwinyi, repulsed by the thought of him seeing me so naked. One of the wild dogs trotted up to me and sniffed my *okuoko*. I heard Mwinyi put the two large rabbits he'd caught down and I assumed the soft yipping I heard was him telling the dogs not to touch the rabbits.

"Can you see?" he asked.

"No," I said.

He clucked his tongue with annoyance. "Get up, Binti."

"I can't." I started crying harder. Then I thought about my *otjize* and my crying turned to sobs. I felt another of the dogs sit on me and I heard Mwinyi walk away. Then I must have fallen asleep because when I woke, I smelled cooking meat. My stomach rumbled and slowly I sat up. The dog who'd sat on me had also apparently fallen asleep and now it lazily stepped off my legs.

I looked around. My world was stable. No expanding, no numbers, no words bouncing, crawling, oozing about with every sound I made. No tunnel in the distance. No feeling like the Earth would hurl me from its flesh into space. I sat back with relief. It was a dark night, the sky overcast with thick clouds. Our camel Rakumi was resting nearby, her saddle on the ground beside her. Mwinyi sat before the fire he'd built, eating. In the darkness, the fire was a welcome beacon. I stood up and then hesitated.

"I'm not Himba," he said, without looking away from the fire. "Your *otjize* looks like adornment to me. You don't look naked. Come and eat. We're not staying here long."

Regardless, as I crept up to him, I burned so hot with embarrassment that I could only approach walking sideways. I sat right beside him. This way, he'd have to make more of an effort to look at me. When I looked up, I noticed the dogs lying on top of one another on the other side of the fire, a pile of small bones beside them.

"Aren't they wild dogs?" I asked.

"Yes," he said.

"So why are they still here?"

He shrugged. "The fire's warm and they like me." He turned to me. Surprised by his sudden look, my eyes grew wide and I crossed my arms over my chest and instinctively tried to pull my head into my top. It was such a silly thing to do that he grinned and laughed. I found myself smiling back at him. He had a nice smile.

He turned back to the fire and said, "And I gave them one of the rabbits I caught."

I laughed, again.

"We made an arrangement," he continued. "I feed them and they stay and stand guard for a few hours while you and I get more sleep."

"They told you this?"

He nodded. "Wild dogs are free and playful, once you convince them not to attack you," Mwinyi said. "I suspect we have until their bellies have settled and our fire dies down. I don't think there are many other dangerous animals out tonight. But Binti, something's clearly happening in your homeland . . . and maybe not just in your homeland."

And what if it's because of me? I thought. Maybe he was thinking it too because he was quiet and pensive and for several minutes neither of us spoke.

I changed the subject. "My best friend Dele . . . well, he

used to be my best friend," I said, gazing into the fire. "Now, I don't think he's a friend at all."

"Sorry to hear that," Mwinyi said.

"It's okay," I said. "I think I lost all my friends when I left, really." We were silent for a moment. I continued, "Dele was always interested in the old Himba ways. He knew everything. He was always reminding me that the Himba see fire as holy. A medium to communicate with the Seven. What was the name . . . *okuruwo,* holy fire. Yes, that was it." I sighed, the warmth of the fire toasting my legs and face. "During Moon Fest, I'd sit beside Dele with the other girls and boys. While everyone else sang, I wanted to dance in front of the fire because I always thought the Seven preferred dance and numbers to singing. After I was tapped to be master harmonizer, Dele said I would be disgracing myself if I danced." I frowned. When I'd last spoken to him, he'd been apprenticed to train as the next Himba chief; he'd looked and spoken to me as if I were a lost child.

"To us Enyi Zinariya, fire is holy too," Mwinyi said.

Something large and green zipped past my ear, zoomed a circle over the fire, and then plunged into it. There was a small burst of sparks and a soft *paff!*

"What was that?" I said, jumping up.

"Sit," Mwinyi said. "And watch."

I didn't sit. But I watched.

A second later what looked like an orange, yellow, red spark the size of a tomato flew from the flames, shooting straight up into the black night sky. Then it silently went out.

"I thought you'd spent time in the desert before," he said.

"Only during the day."

"Ah, that explains why you've never seen an Icarus," he said. "They're large green grasshoppers who like to fly into fires. Then they fly out of the flames and dance with their new wings of fire and fall to the ground wingless. The wings grow back in a few days. Then they do it again. The zinariya says that some woman genetically engineered them as pets long ago."

I looked around for the wingless grasshopper. When I saw the creature, I ran to it. I picked it up and held it to my face. It smelled like smoke. "Ridiculous," I whispered as it jumped from my hand to the sand and hopped wingless into the darkness.

"Can . . . can you harmonize with them? Ask them why they do it?" I asked, coming back to the fire.

"Never bothered. I doubt they know why they do it, really. It's how they were programmed by science, I guess."

"Well, maybe," I said. "But I'm sure they rationalize it somehow."

"True. I'll ask one someday."

I sat down at my spot and as I did, he moved his hands before him and then asked, "How are you feeling?"

"Who wants to know?" I asked.

"Your grandmother."

"Why doesn't she ask me?"

He cocked his head and laughed. Then moved his hands again. Moments later, my world began to expand and I shrieked. The words came at me like a cluster of beasts zooming from the depths of the desert. I thought they were going to smash into me, so I raised my hands to protect myself. Bright like sunshine the words read, "ARE YOU ALRIGHT?"

"Okay," I whispered, still hiding behind my raised hands. "Tell her I am okay."

The words receded, but my world did not stop expanding. I touched the ground, grasping cool sand with my fists and digging my feet into it. I felt better.

"Ariya says don't try to use the zinariya except with me," Mwinyi said. "Give it about a week. You have to ease into it or it'll make you really ill. Focus on what's ahead more than what's behind, for now."

I nodded, rubbing my temples.

"Do you want to hear how I learned I was a harmonizer?" he asked, after a moment.

I nodded, digging my fingers and toes deeper into the sand. Anything to take my mind from the terrible feeling of leaving the Earth.

"When I was about eight years old—"

I gasped. "I was eight when I found my *edan*!" I said. "Is that when you—"

"Binti, I'm telling you the story of it. Just listen."

"Sorry," I said, wishing everything would stop undulating.

"So, when I was eight, I walked out into the desert," he said. "My family was used to me doing this. I never went far and I only went during the day, in the mornings. I would walk until I could not see or hear the village."

I smiled and nodded, the thought taking my mind off my rippling world a bit. I, too, had loved to walk into the desert when I was growing up. Even though I was never supposed to. And doing so changed my life.

"This day, I was out there, listening to the breeze, watching a bird in the sky. I unrolled my mat and sat down on a patch of hardpan. It was a cloudy day, so the sun wasn't harsh. They came from the other side of a sand dune behind me, or maybe I'd have seen them. I hadn't heard them at all! They were that quiet. Or maybe it was something else."

"What? What were 'they'?" I asked. "Another tribe?"

He nodded. "But not of humans, of elephants."

My mouth fell open. "I've never seen one, but I hear they hate human beings! The Khoush say they kill herdsmen and maul small villages on the outskirts of—"

"And they always kill every human being they come across, right?" he asked, laughing.

I pressed my lips together, frowning, and unsurely said, "Yes?"

"Because I'm actually a spirit," he said.

I shivered at his words, thinking, *Is he?*

Mwinyi groaned. "Haven't you learned *anything* from

all this? What'd you think I was a few days ago? What did you think of all Enyi Zinariya?" I didn't respond, so he did. "You thought we were savages. You were raised to believe that, even though your own father was one of us. You know why. And now I'm sitting here telling you how I learned I was a harmonizer and you're so stuck on lies that you'd rather sit here wondering if I'm a *spirit* than question what you've been taught."

I sighed, tiredly, rubbing my temples.

Mwinyi turned to me, looked me up and down, sucked his teeth, and continued, keeping his eyes on me as he spoke. Probably enjoying my discomfort with his gaze. "They rushed up to me," he said. "The biggest one, a female who was leading the pack. She charged at me. When you see elephants coming at you as you sit in the middle of the desert . . . you submit. I was only eight years old and even I knew that. But as she came, I heard her charge, 'Kill it! Kill it!' I looked up and I answered her. 'Why?!' I shouted. She stopped so abruptly that the others ran into her. It was an incredible sight. Elephants were tumbling before me like boulders rolling down a sand dune. I will never forget the sight of it.

"When they all recovered, she spoke to me, again, 'Who are you? How are you able to speak to us?' And I told her. And I told her that I was alone and I was a child and I would never harm an elephant. The others quickly lost interest in me, but that one stayed. She and I spoke that day about tribe and communication. And for many years, we met there when the moon was full, as we agreed. A few times we met when I needed her advice, like when my mother was ill and when I quarreled with my brothers who were bigger and older than me."

"What of your sisters?"

"I don't have any," he said. "I'm the youngest of six, all boys."

"Oh," I said. "That's strange."

"What's stranger is that I'm the only one who doesn't look like he could crush stone with his bare hands," he said, smiling ruefully. "Even Kam, who's a year older than me, just won the village wrestling championship."

I laughed at Mwinyi's outrage.

"Anyway, during these times, when it wasn't a full moon, I was able to call Arewhana, that was her name, from far away. She taught me how to do it. It was something she said I could do with larger, more aware animals like elephants, rhinos, and even whales if I ever ventured to the ocean.

"Arewhana taught me so much. *She* was the one who told me I was a harmonizer. And she was the one who taught me how to *be* a harmonizer. Elephants are great violent beasts, but only because human beings have treated them in a way that made using violence the only way for elephants to survive. There are many elephant tribes in these lands and beyond."

An elephant had taught him to harmonize and instead of using it to guide current and mathematics, she'd taught him to speak to all people. The type of harmonizer one was depended on one's teacher's worldview; I rolled this realization around in my mind as I just stared at him.

Mwinyi's bushy red hair was still full of dust and sand and he didn't seem to mind this, but his dark brown skin was clean and oiled. I'd actually seen him rubbing oil into his skin earlier. I knew the scent. It was from a plant that grew wild in the shade of palm trees and some women used it to flavor desserts because it tasted and smelled so flowery. He carried some in a tiny glass vial he kept in his pocket. A few drops of it went a long way. The oil protected his skin from the desert sun in a way quite similar to *otjize,* and it brought out its natural glow. I wondered if this plant smell had also set the elephants at ease.

I chewed on this thought, while gazing at Mwinyi. My world had stabilized again.

~

As I settled on the mat in the tent, I could hear Mwinyi moving about outside while he softly yipped and panted. I watched as the wild dogs got up; soon our tent was surrounded by the group of about eight dogs. None of them slept now; instead they sat up and watched out into the night like sentries.

Mwinyi came into the tent and lay beside me. "Better sleep now," he said. "I think we have about three hours of safety at most. Then they'll leave and if there are hyenas or bigger angrier dogs out there, *those* can sneak up on us."

He didn't have to tell me twice. Sleep stole me away less than a minute later.

Chapter 2

Orange

Every week, the village market opened in the desert. Always at noon, when the sun was highest in the sky. The village was small, but it wasn't isolated. People came from different villages, towns, communities. But these connected communities were small and all of them were insular, secretive, and happy. And that's why it worked.

The children loved their mobile phones and social networks; some of them ventured out into the rest of the country or even the world. A few never came back. But most stayed and all kept the area's secret. There were never any uploaded photos, drawings, paintings, or videos. No blog posts, no interviews, no news stories. No need to share. The people in this part of the country took from the rest of the world, but kept to themselves and explored from within. The people here preferred to venture inward rather than out. Because what was within was already a million times more advanced, more modern, than anything on the planet. And what was inside had come from outer space. Thus, the rest of the country never learned of the friendly "alien invasion," the friendship that took root and was on full display in the market every week.

Women squatted before pyramids of tomatoes, onions, dried leaves, spices. Men brought in bunches of plantain on their heads, reams of Ankara cloth. The local imam was holding a meeting. Children ran errands and into mischief. And among them all walked twenty-foot-tall, slender beings who seemed to be made of molten gold. They glinted in the sunshine and people sometimes shaded their eyes against the glare, but other than that, these extraterrestrial people mingled easily and naturally.

One girl ran around one of them, stopped, and brought up her hands. She motioned wildly and then kept running. She wove around two women haggling over a yam, squeezed between the group of men listening to the local imam preach, and ran right up to the tall golden figure waiting for her. She smiled, held up an orange whose peel had been cut away. "You bite into it," she said. "Like this."

~

I awoke with the taste of oranges in my mouth. When I opened my eyes, I was facing the desert and I could see the dream that wasn't a dream retreating from me into the distance, like something sneaking away.

"Why bother hiding?" I muttered. "Why don't you just ask if you want to tell me stories? I am a student. I will listen."

I sat up and looked around. The dogs were gone. The sun was about an hour from rising and Mwinyi was already preparing Rakumi for the journey. I sat up and watched him for a moment as he grunted and patted the camel's back before strapping the saddle onto her. There was a strange moment when Rakumi turned and looked right at Mwinyi and he gazed right into her eyes. Then the camel touched her soft lips to his forehead and turned forward and Mwinyi finished putting the saddle on.

I reached for my jar of *otjize* and held it before my eyes. So little left. I applied some to my face and a thin layer to my arms and lower parts of my legs, rubbing some into my anklets. If my family saw me like this, they'd be mortified. At least during more normal times. I climbed out of the tent and stretched my back. I was stiff, but okay, having slept about four solid hours.

"Good morning," I said.

He turned around and nodded. "Not yet, but soon."

"Can we make it there by the end of the day?" I asked.

"Maybe. If we move quickly."

But what will we find? I thought. I shivered and went to relieve myself a distance away from our camp. As I walked back, I called up a current and let myself tree while I looked up at the night sky. There were stars now. The clouds had dissipated. I would see things clearly when I returned home.

I reached into my pocket and brought out the golden ball with the fingerprint-like designs on it. Running a current around its surface, I watched as the ball lifted from my palm and rotated before me like a tiny planet. Then I retracted the current and let the ball drop into my hand.

When I put it back in my pocket, I ran my fingertips over the triangular metal pieces sitting at the bottom.

I reached into my other pocket and brought out my astrolabe. Holding it to my face, I stopped walking. I stared at the elegant device. What I realized made me sick to my stomach and my legs grow weak. After all the changes I'd been through in the last year, becoming part Meduse, making *otjize* on a different planet, but especially with the activation of the zinariya, my astrolabe didn't seem like the most advanced technology anymore. Astrolabes were the only object that also carried the full record of your entire life on it—you, your family, and all forecasts of your future. The chip in it had to be transferred if the astrolabe broke, which they rarely ever did if they were made by my father or me. My family's fortune and identity were based on the importance of astrolabes to the world and beyond and the superiority of the ones we made. Even peoples at Oomza Uni used astrolabes. However, I'd barely even glanced at mine since I'd been taken into the desert.

Now I touched it to turn it on and my heart sank even lower. It wouldn't turn on. I called up a current and used it to "inspire" my astrolabe. I'd built this astrolabe myself, special specific part by special specific part. I'd made it to last. But because I knew every inch of it, I knew that now it was pointless trying to turn it on, reset it, shake it, smash it against my leg. My astrolabe was dead. I whimpered as it crossed my mind that maybe even the chip inside it was now unreadable. This would mean that I'd just lost my entire identity. I put the astrolabe in my pocket and took five deep breaths, the tears in my eyes drying more with each breath. Mwinyi finished packing the tent on Rakumi's back.

"I'm ready when you are, " I told Mwinyi.

~

Rakumi walked at a steady strong pace, her onward wave-like movement seeming to say, "Forward, forward, forward." The motion was uncomfortable at first, but I grew used to it. Mwinyi sat right behind me and I leaned against him and this is how we stayed for several hours.

"Binti?" Mwinyi asked, breaking the silence.

"Yes?"

"We're close."

"I know. The land looks the same but it's somehow familiar."

"I have something to tell you," he said. "From your grandmother."

My astrolabe was broken and in order for my world to stay as it was, I had taken Mwinyi's advice and not tried to use the zinariya at all since going to sleep. I hadn't bothered trying to reach Okwu through my *okuoko,* either. In this way, the last several hours of disconnection had been the most peaceful hours I'd experienced in quite some time. My heart began to pound and suddenly it felt difficult to breathe, and an image of Heru's chest bursting flashed through my mind.

Mwinyi climbed off Rakumi and I did the same. We stood there facing each other.

"What . . . did she say?" I whispered.

He hesitated for several moments and I wanted to hug him for those moments. "Three days after we left your home, you stopped hearing from your partner Okwu."

I frowned at the word "partner." "Yes. I'd just learned I could reach it through a sort of . . . connection we had. I said I was okay, Okwu said it was okay, then that third day, nothing." I turned to Mwinyi and he looked at me as if he wanted to put some distance between us. "Why?" I asked.

"I know more of what happened now," he said. He looked at his feet. "The Ariya told me everything a day ago."

I frowned deeply at him.

Mwinyi looked me in the eye now. "I thought it better to tell you now than a few hours ago."

We stared at each other. Rakumi's reins clicked and dragged on the sand as she looked curiously at us.

"That wasn't your choice to make," I finally said, but the words didn't come out in an angry growl, they came out choked. I pressed the tips of my right fingers to my forehead. "I'd rather know ev—"

"They came for Okwu."

I sighed. "Khoush soldiers," I said. "We know that. They fought and my family fled into the Root, into the cellar. Right?"

"Yes."

It felt as if there were hot embers in my chest. "Okwu . . . Did they . . ." I didn't want to say it. "Tell me, Mwinyi!"

A pained look crossed his eyes and that made everything he said next more devastating. "Things . . . things didn't happen exactly as I thought." He took a deep breath and surprised me by stepping closer. "The Khoush did come for Okwu. They'd always planned to come for it. The Meduse-Khoush War . . ."

"I understand," I snapped. "Go on."

Mwinyi nodded and continued. "Your father said they blew up its tent, but Okwu wasn't in it. Okwu wasn't there. The Khoush soldiers demanded that your family tell them where it was. Your family refused. They threatened to kill your father."

I pressed my hands to my mouth. "They killed my—"

"No, no," he said, taking my wrists. "But your family would not give up Okwu."

I looked into Mwinyi's eyes and said, "If they burned Okwu's tent, that's deep, deep disrespect to Himba land . . . Land is sacred to us. We would never, *ever* cooperate after something like that."

Mwinyi nodded. "This angered the soldiers and they used their weapons to set the Root on fire," Mwinyi said. "And . . ."

I was suddenly faint. "The Himba don't go out, we go in," I said, breathlessly. "My family ran into the Root . . . and the Khoush set it on fire, didn't they? What I saw *was* true!"

Mwinyi kept talking as I paced in circles, my hands grasping my *okuoko*. "Your father believes Okwu killed many of them," Mwinyi said. "Even as the Root was burning with all of them inside, he could hear it. Khoush screaming, over and over. The only Meduse there was Okwu, so it had to be Okwu doing it. And it most likely sent a distress call to other Meduse. But eventually, the noise stopped. All this, your father communicated to your grandmother."

"As the Root was burning around him, around everyone?" I shouted at him.

Mwinyi paused, seeming to question whether or not to say more. "At some point," he continued, "he stopped communicating with her through the zinariya. So Binti, I . . . I don't know what we're going to find when we get there."

"The Ariya knew all this before we left?"

"Yes."

"Yet she told us half-truths and didn't try to stop me from leaving."

"No."

"She would not have succeeded," I muttered. I felt numb. Dead. Mwinyi may not have known what we'd find there, but I did. Charred bones. My family was dead. My family was dead. My family was dead . . . five five five five five five five five five five five. I climbed high into the tree and when I turned to Mwinyi, the motion felt slow, and I could have been looking at him from outer space. "If you think I'm such a mess, why did you come with me?"

His eyebrows rose. "I'm the only one who could get you here safely on my own."

We stared into each other's eyes and I knew he wasn't telling me all of it. I waited. And waited. When it was clear he wasn't going to speak, I blurted, "If Okwu called on its people, it's the Khoush-Meduse War all over again."

He looked away. "Maybe."

"What if no one is left?"

"I don't—"

"You know you don't have to *say* it to say it to me," I said. "And, Mwinyi, I came back with a Meduse, the Khoush nearly killed both of us the minute we stepped off the ship, why would they leave it at that?" I stepped over to Rakumi, my legs feeling like someone else's legs. The number five was in everything and I was glad. I patted Rakumi's neck. "And why would Okwu *not* fight back? It wanted a reason to use the weapons it made at Oomza Uni, the same place the Khoush brought the chief's stinger. Okwu hadn't forgotten anything. And the Khoush have always been jealous of the Himba; why not find a reason to burn down Osemba's oldest home?" I shut my eyes, whispering, "Z = z^2 + c." When my heart rate had decreased, I said, "All because I came home."

"Binti," Mwinyi said. "It wasn't your homecoming, it was a matter of *time*."

I was listening to his every word, from deep in the tree, but in my heart, I burned.

"Ouch!" Mwinyi hissed. I felt the electric shock all over my body, but mainly in one of my *okuoko*. Rakumi bucked and groaned loudly, turning an eye toward us to see what was going on. "Why does your hair do that?"

I frowned, staring ahead. "It's not hair."

"What?"

"When I was on the ship, the Meduse, they did this to me."

"Sorry," he said. "I'm sorry . . . I didn't . . . can I ask you . . . why . . . why did you let them—"

"I didn't *let* them!" I shouted. My eyes were hot with tears. I needed to get home. "But it was done. I couldn't turn back." The world had started exploding again. If I looked behind me, I knew I'd see the tunnel that was often there, the one that led to the alien mind of my other people. I wanted to scream. I was too many things and my family was charred bones in the ruins of my home . . . five five five five five five five. I sat down right there in the sand beside Rakumi's front leg. I climbed higher up the tree and stayed there.

Mwinyi climbed back on Rakumi. Minutes later, I got up and did the same. And for the next hour, we were quiet again. Tears fell from my eyes as I stared at the open desert ahead. I had to drink more water than usual because of it. The number five flew around me like a swarm of gnats at sunset. And behind me loomed the tunnel, I knew. Every so often, I felt Mwinyi shift about as he moved his hands this way and that, speaking to whomever he was speaking to. I didn't care; I wasn't interested in talking to those who were behind us.

~

"What's that?" we both said at the same time. Mwinyi was looking at the stones, I was looking at the smoke.

"Stop!" I screamed. "Oh stop! Rakumi, stop!" When the camel kept walking, I started climbing down. Mwinyi grunted deep in his throat and Rakumi stopped just as my sandaled feet reached the sand. I landed hard and bent low, then I started running. We were still miles away. As I ran, I heard my anklets clicking and I was reminded of the sound of my sisters and mother moving about the Root and of Himba women dancing during Moon Fest.

I stopped among the stones and fell to my knees as I stared. The Root. No, not just the Root, the part of Osemba closest to it too. Burning, crumbling, attacked. Even from here, I could smell the smoke. Billowing up from burning or burned homes and buildings. I could not see exactly what, but I knew Osemba enough to know where things were.

"As we were coming, I was dying," I whispered, my hands pressed to my mouth, my eyes wide and dry as the hot breeze blew. They hadn't just destroyed the Root. They'd taken much of Osemba, too?

I felt Mwinyi's hand on my shoulder as he knelt beside me. I inhaled and exhaled, focusing on each breath, just as my therapist had taught me. I calmed some. "When I first left here," I said quietly, wringing my hands, "I left on a ship called Third Fish. It was . . . *she* was alive."

"Bigger than a whale?" he asked.

"What?"

Mwinyi only shook his head. "Not important. Tell me about your Third Fish."

"Miri 12s," I said, trying to focus on the image of the Third Fish in my mind, instead of what I saw ahead. "They are probably the finest technology, finest *creature,* this planet has ever produced. What else can leave Earth with nothing but itself and travel through space? But *it* all happened in Third Fish. Everyone was killed by the Meduse. I nearly died in there. When I came back here, I happened to get Third Fish again for the journey. I stepped onboard Third Fish and I felt such a . . . comfort. I wish I were on her now, her peacefulness swallows everything bad."

We were at the place where I'd found my *edan*; the group of gray stones jutting out from the ground like flattened old teeth. This was where I had practiced treeing and prepared for my Oomza Uni interviews. The stones were large enough to sit on and arranged in a wide semicircle that opened west, facing my hometown. Mere feet away, beside one of the stones, was the spot where I'd dug up my *edan*.

I looked at this place and suddenly I saw that the ground around it shimmered as if sprinkled with flecks of gold. Mwinyi seemed to see it too. I wasn't ready to stand up, so I crawled there, grinding sand into my red skirt, feeling it enter the bottoms of my sandals as it stripped away the *otjize* on my knuckles. I didn't care about any of it. I sat down at the spot where I'd been, where I'd dug up the *edan,* back when my life had been simple, and looked at the speckled ground. Mwinyi came and stood over me.

"The shimmer isn't physically there," he said. "The zinariya is showing it to us."

I touched the sand where the sparkles were, rubbing it between my fingers. No matter how hard I tried, and no matter how real the gold flecks in the sand looked, I could not touch them.

"It *was* there," he added, kneeling down beside me. "A long time ago." And as if his words cued it to happen, the world expanded again, but this time, I didn't feel as if it would repel me into space. Instead, it was as if the sand around us was disappearing, all of it shifting away, and as it shifted, I . . . we, both Mwinyi and I, lowered. Mwinyi grabbed my arm and I knew that he too was seeing it happen. We both looked around as the stones seemed to grow taller and wider and then their bases became shiny thick very solid gold, as did the ground beneath us. A large imperfect circle about the size of the Root emerged, the semicircle of gold-based stones in the center. I ran a hand over the smooth surface that shined so brightly in the sun we both had to squint and shade our eyes. It was warm.

Mwinyi grasped my arm more tightly and said, "Don't move. It's alright." If he had not done this, I'd have fled for my life, and my confused perspective of what was now and what was decades ago was so skewed, I probably would have run right into one of the stones.

These People had limbs, two arms and two legs, each over twenty feet long and thin like the trunks of palm trees. Their bodies were smooth and long. And they looked made of solid gold. They walked with a slow grace that suggested fluidity. Gold was malleable when it was warm, and they were solar, their form of life might have been energy akin to the currents I could call using mathematics.

They were coming toward the gold plane. They were not slow, but their motions were watery. Had they always been shaped like this, I did not know, for this clearly had been after they'd been around human beings for those few years. The first stepped in the center while the others waited on the sand. It stood up straight and raised its hands above its head. Then its arms then legs fused. I could hear it, soft slurping, ripples running over its flesh as it flattened and smoothed itself out into what looked like a five-foot-high, ten-foot-wide wedge.

The rocks around us began to vibrate and *phoom,* off the golden wedge shot into the sky, so fast that it was gone in seconds. There was no sonic boom, no smoke, not even a gust of air, like with the Third Fish. But high in the sky, I could see a wink of gold, then nothing. The next one stepped onto the platform and did the same.

"These are the Zinariya, the aliens who gave us the zinariya technology," Mwinyi said, awed. "We loved them so much we named our tribe after them. I've never seen them before. Not like this! I've never thought to ask."

"And this was the launch port," I said, as we watched the second one shoot into the sky. When the third one stepped onto the platform, it stopped and turned to us. Mwinyi's hand clenched my arm tighter and we pressed closer to each other. It leaned down and brought forth an arm whose end became a hand with long, long fingers. In its hand was what might have been the golden center of my *edan,* except its surface was smooth, not fingerprint ridged. As Mwinyi and I watched, silver slivers rose from the golden ground, flipped up, and fitted around it, clicking and clacking, until it became the object that I had known until recently. It dumped the *edan* to the ground but instead of falling, it hovered before us. Then the world around us shifted, the sand rose, and the Zinariya people disappeared and we were back where we had been.

"Do you know what that meant?" Mwinyi asked.

I shook my head and was about to say more when a ship zoomed in from the north toward my village. I could see its sleek yellow design. It seemed to land nearby. A Khoush ship in Osemba. Unheard of. I started walking home.

Chapter 3

When Elephants Fight

The Root was still burning.

It was made of stone and concrete; *how* was it on fire? The bioluminescent plants that covered it had burned to ash. The solar panels on the roof had wilted like plants, some of them were probably puddles of synthetic steel in the debris. Six generations of my family had lived here. The Root was the oldest house in my village, maybe the oldest in the city. This was where we had family and community gatherings because the living room was so spacious that it could fit a hundred people.

Powerful Khoush weapons had been shot into it, exploding and then burning so hot that they could even combust and melt stone. All the floors of the Root had collapsed, burned, and smoldered into a heap. Chunks of concrete and rubble blown out when the house exploded were littered around the heap. What remained looked like a giant mound of still smoking blackened char.

"Mama!" I called, walking toward it as I looked around wildly. I coughed as smoke wafted in my direction. "Papa!" I stopped yards away, everything around me was silent but the sound of embers crackling and softly popping. I looked away. Then, slowly, I turned to face what was left of my home. *Because of me,* I thought. And I could feel my *okuoko* begin to writhe on my head and against my back. My Meduse anger sharpened everything. The Khoush had always seen my people as expendable, tools to use, toy with, and discard, useful animals until we weren't useful anymore. During war, we were just in the way.

"*When elephants fight, the grass suffers.*" The green words appearing before me seemed so out of place and the words so profound that I was snapped from my dark thoughts. Mwinyi had sent them to me through the zinariya.

My eye went to the base of the house where the embers were glowing.

"It wasn't just called the Root because it was a family place," I said. "Most of the house's foundation was actually built on the old root of an Undying tree." My mother had told me this when I was about five years old. I'd been sure she was just joking until the next thunderstorm when I realized the house wasn't groaning because of the wind. "The cellar was—" I couldn't say it. I knew what we'd find in the cellar.

Mwinyi left me and walked around the house.

As I stood there, I felt it more than I heard it and every part of me reacted. My *okuoko* writhed, one of them actually slapping the side of my face as if to say, "Look!" The zinariya contracted and expanded my world and I heard distant voices commenting from a distant place, just softly enough for me not to understand. I automatically called the simple equation that always focused my mind, $a^2 + b^2 = c^2$. Then over and over, I spoke the number that relaxed me, "Five, five, five, five, five, five, five." I let my mind follow the zipping dancing fives and with each triangular motion, I steadied. When I looked toward the road leading to the Root, I was thankfully calm enough to simply observe what stood there like the spirit it was.

The Night Masquerade. Again. This time during the *day*! And now I was seeing it from much closer than I had the first time when I stood in my bedroom a few days ago, before my bedroom had been burned to ash. It looked taller, standing about my father's height. Its raffia body cracked and snapped as it stretched an arm to point its long finger at me, fingers of gnarled sticks. The wooden mask's mouth was full of yellow teeth.

Only men were supposed to see the Night Masquerade and it was believed its appearance signified the approach of a big change; whether it brought change with its presence or change came afterward was never clear. The Night Masquerade was the personification of revolution. Its presence marked heroism. To also see it during the day was doubly unheard of. My family was dead; what more change could I endure? What was heroic about this happening? If this was a revolution, it was an awful one.

It spoke in Otjihimba and its voice was like the sound of a vibrating Undying tree during a thunderstorm. "Death is always news," it said, the acrid smoke billowing from its head thickening.

I felt the world swim around me as the weight of my family's death and my own terror tried to pull me down. Around it, everything seemed to vibrate. My eyes watered, and I kept blinking and blinking away the blurriness. The Night Masquerade slowly stepped toward me and I nearly screamed. Instead, I coughed as I inhaled a great whiff of its smoke.

"A bird who has flown off the earth and then returns to land is still on the land," it said. "Remove your shoes and listen."

Phoom! The smoke from its head was copious now and when it finally cleared, the Night Masquerade was gone.

"Oh, thank the Seven," I whispered. But its presence stayed with me and its words echoed in my mind. I looked down at my dusty sandals. I'd bought them on Oomza Uni in the local market. They were made from the secretions of a friendly spider that lived in swamps. When fresh, the webbing could be molded into anything. When it dried, it kept that shape for a thousand years, the seller told me.

I was considering taking them off when Mwinyi called, "Binti. Come here."

He and Rakumi were on the other side of the house and as I jogged there, I felt faint. My family was in the cellar. Dead. Had they burned? Suffocated first? "We cannot get out," my father had said. I stopped and realized that beside me were the charred remains of the sandstorm analyzer my brother had built and placed on the roof. The steel box with its optical particle counters looked like the discarded head of a primitive robot. He'd been so proud of that instrument and so had my mother.

As I ran around the side of the house, I stopped again. My mouth fell open. Then I shut it because I could taste the stench through my mouth just as much as I could smell it through my nose. There were bodies all over and vultures stood and were pecking at some of them. Khoush soldiers. Men and women. With their chests burst open. I twitched and I was back on the ship in the middle of space. The smell of blood and now decay. *How is that possible?* I thought, because my stunned senses were telling me I was alone on the Third Fish again and the Meduse had just performed *moojh-ha ki-bira*. It had just happened.

Happened.

No warning.

So many.

I saw stars. Red and blue and silver. Bursting before my eyes. My mouth was full of decay, as it hung open, trying to pull in air. Now I couldn't breathe. None around me were breathing. I stumbled, gasping, and one of the vultures lazily spread its wings and hopped away.

I blinked and I was back at the remains of the home where I'd been born. The violence was here now. I'd brought it by leaving home and coming back home. I was hyperventilating now. *What did my therapist Saidia Nwanyi say I should do when I can't breathe?* I thought. I put my hands behind my head, though doing so made me feel more exposed to the gruesome sight before me. There had to be fifteen, maybe even twenty bodies strewn about like fallen trees. "Five, five, five, five, five," I chanted as I let myself tree. Each time the number left my lips, I was able to take in more breath. And with each breath, I came back to myself. The moment I could move, I fled.

When I reached the back of the house, I stepped onto a sheet of solid yellow glass. It cracked and shattered beneath my foot. I took another step and stopped, realizing this was the spot where Okwu's tent had been. Mwinyi stood in the blackened center. Not far to the left was what remained of my brother's garden, a charred skeleton of tomato bushes and ash. Rakumi sniffed the greener parts and began munching on a tomato bush.

"Did you see—"

"Yes," he said, still looking at the cracking glass beneath him.

"I think Okwu did that," I said.

"Maybe because the Khoush did this," he stamped on the glass and his sandal went right through it, shards flying this way and that.

I shut my eyes and took deep breaths, holding myself shallowly in the tree, numbers and equations cartwheeling and floating around me. "This explosion would have killed anything it hit," I said. "Unless Okwu wasn't in the tent."

"I don't think they killed it," Mwinyi said.

"Why?"

"Your family was hiding inside the Root when they set it on fire." He paused to inspect my face. "They burned the Root because they couldn't find you or . . . or Okwu."

The idea hit me so hard that when I turned and ran off, I didn't care about the possibility of glass cutting my feet through my sandals.

The road into town was dusty and my sandals kicked it up with every step. Even as I ran further and further from home, the air continued to smell of smoke. The Yennes' house was still burning. The Mahangu building was blown to bits. The Omuzumbas' house was still intact and I glimpsed someone on the balcony watching me run by. How many others were watching me run down the road? How many had fled the destruction?

A Khoush ship had just flown by, which meant they were still in the area. I didn't care. I passed the remains of the souq, where it looked as if the market's women and men had left everything behind in a rush. There were overturned tables and booth dividers and in some places crushed and rotten meat, vegetables, piles of grains, and crushed baskets. The smell of spices, snuff, and incense mixed with the stench of smoke here. I leapt over an overturned bench. Sweat was pouring down my face now, and my heart felt like it would smash through my chest.

I stopped at the lake and stood there. Its water was so serene that it looked like the glass burned into the sand where Okwu's tent used to be. "So calm in all this chaos," I said, breathing hard. The sweat was getting into my eyes, so I wiped my hand down my face. My hand came away red orange with *otjize*. I heard someone behind me.

"What . . . are . . . you doing?" Mwinyi asked, jogging up. He bent forward to catch his breath, putting his hands on his knees. "We don't know if the Khoush are around here!"

"I . . . saw the Night Masquerade again," I said. "In broad daylight. We don't know *anything* anymore."

"Back at the Root?" he asked. Even Enyi Zinariya people believed in the Night Masquerade.

I nodded. There was movement to my right and I turned my head. Two men. Himba. I knew them. I knew most everyone in my village. The Council Elder Kapika and his second wife Neeka.

"Binti?" Chief Kapika said, coming closer. Neeka followed. And as they came closer, I noticed more people peeking from behind market dividers and from within homes across the street.

I hesitated, then turned to the water and walked into it. I felt all eyes on me as the lake water washed off the thin layer of *otjize* on my legs and sweat washed it from my face, neck, and arms. In front of all these people, Himba people. I went in up to my waist, then I opened my mouth and shouted, "*Okwuuuuuuuuu!*"

My voice echoed across the water and then there was silence. I could hear people behind me whispering. Still, I waited.

And then the water began to ripple as Okwu swam up

and rose before me. I smiled, tears stinging my eyes. Its dome was a deep blue in the sunshine. And it was covered with clusterwink snails. I stepped back as more domes emerged around it. More Meduse. A woman screamed from the group of people and there was the sound of scuffling feet as people fled.

I waded back to the land, joining Mwinyi. "How did you know?" he asked. He sounded more than nervous, but he didn't step away as the Meduse emerged from the water.

"Because I know Okwu," I said, turning to Okwu. In Meduse, I asked it, "Are you alright?"

"Yes."

"Why didn't you answer me?"

"I didn't want you to come."

"I thought you were dead!" I said.

"It's better than you being dead, Binti."

"W— . . . what happened? Why is . . . The Root! They burned it! And there were dead soldiers. Many! What happened?" I was shaking and crying now.

Okwu blew out gas and both Mwinyi and I started coughing.

"When you left, I stayed in my tent," he said in Otjihimba. "Your family was kind to me, except for your sisters, who like to yell. Your family had a meeting that evening, so many were there. The Khoush came in the night when your father took me out in the desert to meet with your elders in private. The elders wanted to speak with me. And as we talked, from where we were we saw the Khoush ship fly in and blow up my tent."

"What?" I whispered.

"The elders told me to stay with them in the dark, as your father ran back, shouting at the Khoush to stop. He told all your people to run inside for safety. There were Khoush on the ground at this point. One of the Khoush argued with your father. I could hear it; the man called himself General Staff Kuw and he had no hair or *okuoko* on his head. He didn't think I was in the tent and he wanted to know where I was. Your father refused to tell him and the general accused him of sympathizing with the enemy and having a daughter who'd even mated with a Meduse—"

"Mated?" I exclaimed. The Meduse hovering around Okwu all thrummed their domes.

"Yes, the Khoush are a stupid people," Okwu said. "Your father said they were the enemy because they'd just blown up part of his property. This angered General Kuw. That's when he ordered his soldiers to firebomb the Root. I think they expected everyone to run out. They didn't expect your father to run inside as it was burning. But that's what he did and no one came out."

"The Himba do not run away, we run within," I said, quietly. "They went inside, even as it was burning." I clucked my tongue, as my hands began to shake and my mind tried to cloud. "The Khoush like to joke that we are a suicidal people."

"As the elders watched the Root burn in the night, I left them . . . who just stood there staring at the fire that was so huge, it showed light far into the desert," Okwu continued. "As the Khoush, in a stupid rage, went on to firebomb more homes in Osemba. They weren't even looking for me. I activated my armor, crept up to those standing near the house, and killed as many of them as I could. I wanted to kill that General Kuw, but he had already fled onto a ship. Coward.

"For you, for your family, they all deserved to die. When I could kill no more, I covered the air and escaped as they coughed. There were too many who were coming from their ship. One does not fight a war it cannot win. I hid in the lake and waited for the others. Now when the time comes, we will fight the war we will win."

"They burned everything!" I heard Kapika yell from behind me. He pushed his wife away as she tried to hold him back. Several of the people had come back to listen too. "The Khoush came and burned everything! Out of spite! Because of you people!"

There were about ten Meduse and the only one who was not blue floated up so quickly that I thought it would barrel over me. It was so clear that I could see the white of its stinger as the sun shined right through it. The Meduse chief.

"See what they did to Okwu? You see why we kill them?" the chief rumbled. "We have come. They don't know we are here. We will meet them when they are not ready."

I stepped back and looked at them all. "You need to make peace," I said.

"No," the chief said. "We are here. We will make war. You should *want* war."

I felt my *okuoko* twitch as it dawned on me. I looked beyond the Meduse, at the lake. I moaned. I turned to Mwinyi, then to the Himba standing around us. "Chief Kapika," I said, stepping over to him. I put my chin to my chest as I took his hands. I felt him twitch, wanting to pull away from me. My *otjize* had washed off. I stood before him, before *everyone,* naked, so I was not offended by his discomfort. "Please," I said. "I know I come to you as a barbarian. Please, put that aside for now, and focus on the fact that I am a Himba daughter, regardless of how I look and where I have been . . ."

"And what pollutes you," he added.

I paused, restraining my Meduse prideful anger. I let myself tree and called up a current. As the numbers flew around me, through me, I felt calmer, clearer, and more confident, though the anger still boiled beneath, trying to push thoughts of my dead family to the forefront of my mind. I continued to hold his hands, my head respectfully bowed. "Yes, what pollutes me. But I am still a master harmonizer," I said in a steady voice, loudly enough for the others to hear. "I am more than and better than what I was when I left here. I want to call an urgent meeting of the Council Elders." I looked up into his eyes. "It is urgent and a matter of peace in these lands. Please. We can't have more die." I hesitated and then pushed on. "C— . . . call an *Okuruwo*."

An *Okuruwo* was only called when the lifeblood of the Himba people was in grave danger. It was only called by elders, because it was to call on the soul of the Himba to heal itself and that took a power only the old could wield. Usually. The healing power of the Himba is carried within the elders, even the word *Okuruwo* is usually only spoken by older Himba. Thus, the word felt hot coming out of my mouth. I cleared my throat as we stared at each other. His irises were a deep brown, the whites of his eyes yellowed by the sun. "Have you not looked around?" he asked in his soft voice. "Your childish *selfish* actions led to all this strife. We don't leave our lands for a reason, Binti. Now you speak beyond your years. What makes you think *you* can call an *Okuruwo*?"

I didn't miss a beat. "Because there are Meduse ships in the lake and if we don't do something immediately, we'll be the grass crushed beneath the feet of two fighting elephants."

~

The Council Elders use the same method of communication that Himba women use to spread the word about the date of the pilgrimage: a large leaf is cut from a palm tree and passed from member to member. The Himba people are the creators and makers of astrolabes, devices of communication. However, the Himba people have been communicating important meeting announcements in this old, old way for centuries and we will continue to do so.

So I watched a young girl climb a palm tree, use a large machete to cut a large leaf, climb down, and hand it to Chief Kapika. Okwu, Mwinyi, and I stood there silent as he took it and went into his home and came out with a jar of his wife's *otjize*. He held the jar out to me.

"You're calling the *Okuruwo,* so you draw the circle."

"Why don't Himba males put *otjize* on their skins?" Okwu asked, floating up beside me.

From behind me, Mwinyi chuckled. I took the leaf and the jar, ignoring Okwu's question.

"What reason does a man have to be beautiful?" Chief Kapika asked as he watched me spread the leaf on the dry dirt.

"Beauty does not need a reason," Okwu responded.

I opened the jar. The *otjize* was so fragrant that for a moment, I swooned. It had been so long since I'd smelled Earth-made *otjize*. The zinariya squeezed and expanded my world as images of home tried to flood my brain—town's square, the lake, the schoolhouse . . . his wife must have collected the clay from near there. *My* otjize *no longer even smells like this,* I thought.

"You will never understand us," Chief Kapika said dismissively to Okwu.

I drew the circle with *otjize* and handed him the leaf.

He looked at the circle and then at me. "Make sure the Meduse stay in the water," he said. "We will meet and try to make this better." He looked at Okwu, but spoke to me. "*Their* tribesman is alive, there is no reason for war. They have destroyed enough."

"That is not for you to decide," Okwu said. "Unprovoked aggressive action is reason for war."

"The Khoush killed my family," I added flatly. "For we, Himba, that should be an act of war, shouldn't it?"

"I'm sorry, Binti," Chief Kapika said, touching my shoulder. "But if you chose to mingle with the Meduse and if your family chose to welcome one into its home, even built a home for it, why should the rest of us—"

"Because we are Himba!" I shouted, clenching my fists. "Osemba is my home!"

He waved his hand. "Save it for the *Okuruwo,*" he said. "I won't speak for the council." He rolled the palm leaf up and began to walk away. He stopped and turned back to me. "When you come, please apply *otjize*. Use what I gave you, if you have none. You look like a savage." He gave Mwinyi a foul look.

I shot a glance at Mwinyi, who glared at Chief Kapika but held his tongue. When Chief Kapika was out of hearing range, Mwinyi said, "And that's why we will not come to fight for the Himba."

I bit my lip. "He only knows the little we know here," I said. "Forgive him for that."

Mwinyi only looked away, moving his hands smoothly

as he turned his back to me. I didn't ask who he was speaking to.

"Are all your people so afraid?" Okwu asked.

I glared at it.

"I think we should leave here," Mwinyi said, turning back to me. "The conflict between the Meduse and the Khoush is old. It's a large part of why the Enyi Zinariya have stayed away from these lands. Binti, it's not your fault. This was all going to start again, sooner or later. You did what you could on that ship, but even you had to have known it was temporary."

But was it, I wondered. Things had been peaceful all my life and well before that. The pact had held. And in that time, the Himba had flourished. My father was able to build up his shop. Many of us traveled regularly to Khoush cities to sell our astrolabes. Even all that had happened on the Third Fish and with the stinger on Oomza Uni would have remained planets away if I had not been there. No, I had disturbed all of that when I decided to do what we Himba never do.

"I have to try and make it better," I said. "I can't just leave here." *My family,* I thought. Almost all of my loved ones had burned alive and were now charred remains in the Root, the home in which we'd all grown up—my mother, father, siblings, cousins, nieces, nephews, family friends. I shuddered, reaching into my pocket and touching the golden ball of my *edan*. It felt warm and I grasped it. The feeling of its grooved surface was instantly soothing, the feel of the numbers running through my mind as I lightly treed such a relief that my legs felt weak.

I sighed and walked over to a market bench and sat down. "Where is Rakumi?" I flatly asked.

Mwinyi pointed up the road toward the Root. I nodded. "Are you alright?" He sat beside me.

"No," I said. "I will never be alright again."

Okwu glided over to us. "Shall I go with you?" it asked.

I thought about it for a moment. I nodded. "Yes," I said. "For now, though, go back to the chief and the other Meduse and keep them from showing themselves."

"Have the Khoush returned here?" Mwinyi asked.

"They will, " Okwu said and it sounded almost hungry at the prospect. "They are still searching for me. Soon they will realize that I have been hiding in plain sight." Its dome vibrated. Laughter. "You should hope this meeting is successful. Otherwise, tomorrow, there will be war."

Mwinyi looked at me. "When will . . ."

"*O . . . O . . .*" I paused. The word was still hard for me to speak. "*Okuruwo* are always held at sunset," I said. " 'When the fire and the sky are in agreement.' "

~

Mwinyi and I stayed in the empty souq for much of the day, then Mwinyi went back to the Root to get Rakumi; I didn't want to go with. Okwu had returned to the lake, where it quickly disappeared into the water. Once, while in there, it had reached out to me through my *okuoko* and asked, *Are you alright?*

"I am here," I responded.

Mwinyi returned with Rakumi, who must have eaten her fill of what was left of my brother's garden. The camel sat down beside my unrolled mat and went to sleep. The remaining Himba in the area who hid in their homes kept their distance. Once in a while, I could see people walking in small groups up or down the road. People looked our way but quickly moved on.

I spent those few hours resting on my mat, my golden ball levitating before me as I treed. I left the other pieces in my pocket. Somehow, they no longer felt like part of the *edan* anymore. They were like bits of shed skin. I wondered if the golden ball was still poison to Okwu, or if it was just the outer silver-looking pieces. The golden ball had the same tang of the pieces when I touched it to my tongue. "It's not really a good time to ask Okwu," I whispered to myself, and I watched the golden ball rotate before me. The current I sent around it was like an electrical atmosphere around a small planet.

Mwinyi sat beside me, watching for a bit, and other times getting up and walking along the edge of the lake. At one point, he stopped and stood with his back to the lake and looked toward the sky. He stayed like this for nearly an hour. I watched him, while deep inside a flow of mathematics, the golden grooved ball slowly rotating before me, my mind clear, sharp, calm, and distant. Mwinyi's face was peaceful, his lips seemed to be saying something, his hands to his sides, his light blue garments fluttered in the wind, and he stood on the discarded shells of the clusterwink snails who lived in the lake.

I wondered what he was doing. A harmonizer knows when a fellow harmonizer is harmonizing. Who was he speaking to? Maybe the Seven. Eventually, he roused himself, then moved his hands for several minutes. He came back to me and sat on his mat. "Was it a good conversation?" I asked him.

He chuckled, rolled his eyes, and said, "You wouldn't believe it."

I went back to working with the golden ball. If he didn't want to tell me, I was fine with that. Maybe he'd been speaking with my grandmother, or the Ariya, or maybe his parents or brothers. It wasn't always my business.

~

At sunset, I breathed a sigh of relief. The Khoush military hadn't returned. This meant there was still a chance that an *Okuruwo* would help the Himba organize, and maybe I could get us to serve as mediator between the Khoush and Meduse and prevent all-out war. If war intensified between the Khoush and Meduse, if more Meduse came and more Khoush from farther lands came, the fighting would spread and even bleed into other peoples' business. All because of me. On the Third Fish, I had accidently found myself in the middle of something. This time I *was* that middle.

We packed up and Mwinyi and I ate a large meal of leftover roasted desert hare, dried dates, and ground roots. I stepped behind one of the booths and used most of the remaining *otjize* I had to cover myself with a thick layer, rolling my *okuoko* with so much of it that one would not be able to tell that they weren't hair but *okuoko,* tentacles.

I sent a message to Okwu that it was time to go and it emerged from the water less than a minute later. There was an odd moment when Okwu glided up to Mwinyi and they both stayed like that for about thirty seconds. Something passed between them, I was sure. Though Mwinyi had no *edan* or *okuoko,* he was still a harmonizer; where I used mathematics, he used some other form of access to speak with various peoples.

As we left, heading further down the dirt road, I couldn't shake the feeling that from all the sand brick homes and buildings that still stood (once we were a few minutes' walk further from the Root, there was no further Khoush damage), people were watching us. They all must have known about the *Okuruwo* by this time, the news traveling rapidly by astrolabe and word of mouth as the palm leaf was passed from council member home to council member home. And if I knew my people as well as I knew I did, they were hopeful for my success even as they raged at me.

~

The stone building where the council regularly met was on the other side of Osemba, about a two-mile walk. We went around the lake and then set onto the main dirt road. Here, people stared from doorways, windows, and even came out of their homes to look at me, the "one who'd abandoned her people," or Okwu, a "violent Meduse," or Mwinyi, a "savage desert person."

"Why let so many of those grow here?" Mwinyi asked as we passed a large group of trees with thick rubbery leaves and wide trunks covered in hard sharp thorns. He held up his hands and made several motions. A woman standing in the doorway of a large stone house we were passing gasped when she saw this, grabbed her staring toddler, pulled him inside, and slammed her door.

"The Undying trees?" I said, glancing at the closed door. Mwinyi didn't pay the woman any mind. "We couldn't dig them up even if we wanted to, their roots go too deep. Plus, because of them, we found drinkable underground water sources for Osemba; because of them, we can live here. We built our water systems around them."

"I can see children accidentally impaling themselves on them while playing games in your street," Mwinyi said. "Why are they called 'undying'? Do spirits live in them?"

"Spirits live in everything," Okwu said.

"Because they're older than the Himba," I said. "We

respect them. When there are thunderstorms, it's like they come to life. They vibrate. Fast enough to make a howling sound. You have to see it happen to know how incredible it is. And they make this salt that you can scrape from the leaves that'll cure all kinds of sicknesses."

Mwinyi was moving his hands fast now and when he finished by making a pushing motion forward, I saw the air before him warp for a moment. My head ached and I turned to look ahead of us until it stopped.

"Who are you talking to?" I asked.

"Your grandmother," he said. "You know how she loves plants. These will blow her mind." He paused. Then he chuckled. "She knows of them already."

I smiled then I coughed, Okwu's gasp billowing all around me. I heard footsteps scrambling away. When I looked back, I saw a group of children hiding behind the Undying trees, several of them giggling.

"They're just curious," I told Okwu in Meduse, hoping the low rumbly vibration of the language would scare the young girls off. It didn't.

"One of them touched my *okuoko,*" Okwu rumbled back. The children fled at the sound of its Meduse voice. "If they want death by stinger, I will give it to them."

"Remember," I said, switching back to Otjihimba. I smiled. "My *otjize* healed your *okuoko*. The little girl who touched you was covered with *otjize*. She can't be bad for you."

"Her *otjize* would burn my flesh," Okwu rumbled in Meduse, irritably.

"If she touched you, then her *otjize* is on your *okuoko,*" I said, laughing. "I smell nothing burning."

"Your people are rude," Mwinyi suddenly snapped. He was glaring at three men standing at the front of a building laughing. One of them pointed at Mwinyi and opened and closed his hand. "Crude, rude people."

I grasped his arm and pulled him along. "I apologize on their behalf," I said.

"Small-minded insular people," he muttered. "I can speak their language, they can't even greet me in mine." Thankfully, he let me pull him along. I didn't allow myself to think about what they must have been saying about me all this time. And now that there was Khoush-Meduse violence again that had led to the destruction of part of Osemba, and here I was bringing a Meduse to the town's most sacred space, those sentiments would surely worsen. But in our walk across Osemba, though more kids and a few adults taunted Okwu and several spat and shouted at Mwinyi, not one person spoke to me.

~

The Osemba House was a giant smooth dome made of sandstone that sat on the eastern edge of town. The Root was on the westernmost edge, so the two buildings were as far from each other as one could get and still be in Osemba.

The Osemba House was built between three Undying trees and inside was a stone platform built around the Sacred Well.

Daily, women from this side of Osemba came to collect water to drink, for the water here had a refreshing taste and settled upset stomachs in a way that the water pumped around town from the underground river did not. My mother would venture to this side of town once in a while and when she brought home the strange water, we'd all fight each other for our tiny cup of it that we'd sip after dinner. In the back, the outdoor meeting grounds faced the open desert.

"Let's go around," I said. "That's where they'll be." I wasn't sure how anyone would tolerate the three of us, tainted individuals by Himba standards, walking so close to the Sacred Well.

Okwu stopped for a moment and seemed to contemplate the building. When I turned to look at it, I laughed despite everything. "The Himba are a passive-aggressive people," it said in Meduse.

I nodded. "We have ways of making our point strongly without saying a word." It was only now, after being so close to a Meduse, that I gazed upon the Osemba House and realized it looked very much like a Meduse, the enemy of a people who treated the Himba like intelligent slaves. *Everything is so complicated and connected,* I thought. *Everything. And nothing is coincidence, or so my mother used to always say.* The space between my eyes stung. *"Used to." No longer.* I walked faster.

Before I came around the side of the building, I heard the fire. The Sacred Fire was always burning, but only when an *Okuruwo* was called was it grown to this size. They all turned. They had all been waiting for us. Five old men, including Chief Kapika, two old women, including Titi—the woman who led the pilgrimage into the desert—and one young man.

I sighed, my eyes meeting the young man's eyes. It was Dele, my best friend who'd stopped being my best friend when I snuck away to attend Oomza Uni. Who over the last year had decided to grow a beard and was tapped to become an apprentice to Chief Kapika. I had spoken to him just before the Enyi Zinariya came for me. He'd contacted my astrolabe. We'd spoken briefly and he'd looked at me with a pity so painful I'd been glad when the conversation was over. The last thing he'd said to me was, "I can't help you, Binti."

They all sat around the fire, the men wearing deep red kaftans and pants and the women wearing clothes similar to mine, a red wraparound skirt and a stiff red top. Both Titi and the other women had *otjize* rolled locks, braided into tessellating triangle patterns and extending down their backs. Dele's head was shaven on both sides, the dense hair on top twisted into a thick braid that extended behind his head like a horn, stiff with a thin layer of *otjize*.

"Come," Chief Kapika said.

Okwu's voice came to me as if it were thrown. *I don't like fire,* it said.

I approached the Himba Council. *It won't hurt you if you don't get too close,* I responded. *Stay behind me.* I glanced at Mwinyi and he gave me a brief nod. I led the way, Mwinyi behind me and Okwu behind him. I still wore my pilgrimage outfit that my mother had bought me. Fine, fine clothes for one of the finest moments in my life. But now the red skirt was caked with sand and my stiff top was dirty with my own sweat and old *otjize*. And my family was dead.

They sat around the Sacred Fire, Dele on the other side, beside Chief Kapika and another man, the two women on both sides of me, Titi to my right. I took a seat in the space made for me, completing the circle, and Mwinyi and Okwu settled behind me.

I lowered my head. "I'm honored that the Himba Council has answered my call for this . . . *Okuruwo,*" I said, speaking the word a bit too loudly as I pushed it from my lips. "Thank you."

"The council recognizes its daughter," all of them responded. Except Dele, who said nothing. But he was not here as an elder, so he could not speak as one.

"Binti," Chief Kapika began. "You left us like a thief in the night, abandoning your family—"

"I didn't 'abandon' my family," I insisted.

"You gathered us here tonight, small woman," Titi snapped at me. "Don't interrupt an elder."

I fought my indignation and the others waited to see if I could control myself. I exhaled a long breath and lowered my eyes.

"You abandoned your family," Chief Kapika repeated. "Like a thief in the night. For your own needs. Nearly died for your decision and were forced to accept a partnering with the Meduse in order to survive." He paused, looking at the others. "But blood is thicker than . . . water. Like a good Himba, you came home. But you brought the enemy of a people who sees us as less than they are. And when the Khoush came for it, they came for us, too. Now there is war in our homes and around our lands again. Instigated by the actions of one of our own, you. Your lineage here is dead and you've bonded with the savage other part of your bloodline . . . why shouldn't we simply run you out of Osemba?"

I looked up sharply. Angry. "Because the Himba do not turn their own out. We go inward. We protect what is ours by embracing it," I said. "Even when one's bloodline is . . . dead." I paused, the rage and the sight of the roaring fire making me feel more powerful. I stood up before the Sacred Fire. "I left because I wanted more," I said. "I was not leaving my family, my people, or my culture. I wanted to *add* to it all. I was born to go to that school and when I got there, even after everything that happened, that became even clearer. I fit right into Oomza Uni.

"But I had to come home, too. I need it all, you, school, space. I wanted to go on my pilgrimage in order to align myself . . . but it wasn't my path." I paused, to gather my thoughts. "Okwu is my friend . . . yes, fine, my partner. So I also wanted to show it my home. I guess I wanted to open things up here, too. Harmonize the Khoush, Meduse, and Himba"—I motioned to Mwinyi—"and now the Enyi Zinariya, too." I turned back to the fire. "This is why I called this gathering. There's been terror and death and destruction, but I want to pull harmony out of that now. We can." I looked at each of their frowning faces. "Dele," I said, looking straight at him. He jumped a little, surprised. "You know me better than everyone here. You know my heart. You know how much I love everyone and how much I will give to protect and make everyone happy. Hear what I am about to ask."

I pointed in the direction of the lake and said, "Right now as we speak, the Meduse wait in the lake."

Every single council member gasped.

"Binti, no!" Dele exclaimed. "That can't be true!"

"Eh!" one of the elders I didn't know exclaimed. "At this moment?"

"Yes," I said. "There's a ship hiding in the water. Maybe more than one." I let my words sink in. Dele continued staring at me with wide eyes as the others whispered among themselves.

"Your people are not the type to survive war," Okwu said from behind me in Otjihimba.

I heard Mwinyi chuckle.

"The Khoush tried to kill a Meduse, despite the pact, despite Okwu being a *peaceful* ambassador who'd come to Khoushland in peace," I said. "Oomza Uni gained permission from both the Khoush government and Meduse chief for Okwu to come here. And the Khoush burned my home, k-killing my family when they could not find and kill *me,* an honorary Meduse. The Meduse have reason to start war. And the Khoush want it, too. And they will fight over Osemba and Khoushland will burn and broil again. Unless we Himba meet with both sides and stop them." Then I asked what I hadn't even told Mwinyi or Okwu about because they weren't Himba and thus could never understand. "Please, call on the Himba deep culture."

"No!" Titi suddenly shouted.

"Please," I said, barely able to believe what I was doing, what I was saying. A year and half ago, I could never have imagined I'd be right here in this moment. Deep culture goes deeper than what it is, it goes deeper than culture, it crosses over. It communes with the mathematics that dwell within all things and only the collective of Himba Councils could evoke it.

"We will *not*! Who are you to ask that?" Titi snarled, disgusted. She took a deep breath, composing herself. When she spoke again, she was much calmer. "This isn't our fight, Binti. We pack up and go to the pilgrimage grounds and wait there until the Khoush and Meduse exhaust or kill themselves. We bring all our astrolabe supplies, all of our valuables, we go nomad as we were so long ago and we stay together, until this is over!"

"I've . . . I've seen the Night Masquerade," I admitted. "Again. In the day. Don't you have to listen to me?"

Silence, as everyone turned to look at Chief Kapika, as

if waiting for him to say something. Chief Kapika only shook his head, refusing to speak on this subject. Again, I heard Mwinyi chuckling behind me. He seemed to be enjoying this more than everyone else here. "These people don't understand anything," he muttered.

In the silence, Dele suddenly got up and came to me. He stood over me and looked down. "Get up, Binti." When I did, he roughly grabbed my shoulder. "Come on."

Mwinyi was already up. "Where are you taking her?" he demanded. "I'm coming too." Okwu also floated to us.

"Stay here," Dele said, holding up a hand. "Talk to them. Say what you can. She's safe. I just need to speak with her."

"Binti?" Mwinyi asked, looking at me. "Alright?"

"I'll be fine," I said. *And I can call Okwu if I need help,* I said with my eyes. As if he understood, he nodded and stepped back.

Then Dele was pushing me toward the Osemba House back entrance. I glanced behind me at Okwu and Mwinyi, but Mwinyi was facing the still shocked and confused-looking council and saying, "My name is Mwinyi and I'm from the desert and I guess I'm representing the Enyi Zinariya. From what I know . . ."

Then we were inside and Dele was leading me to the Sacred Well in the center of the dome. "What is wrong with you?" he asked. He looked down at me. When had he gotten so much taller?

"What's . . ." I froze when I looked into his dark eyes. They were glistening with tears. I'd known Dele practically all my life. Even when we were small children, I'd never seen Dele cry. Never.

"You saved yourself before," he said. "Do you want to die now?"

"If we don't do something, we'll all die," I said. "The Khoush had to have detected when the Meduse came. They let them so they can attack from the ground. They're flying about looking for the Meduse now. There's not time for us to get out of here before it starts. Not with our things. We'll die in that desert if we leave now."

"The Night Masquerade has shown itself to you, a *girl,* twice! And the second time, it couldn't even wait for the night! You need to stop! You bring chaos," he said. "I shouldn't . . . s—" He looked away.

I stepped back from him. Staring. I knew what he'd meant to say, "I shouldn't even be speaking to you." I should have been dead to him already, for traditionally a woman who ran away from home was useless. And one who saw the Night Masquerade no longer existed. I was a ghost to him, a spirit.

"They have taught you well," I said. "Rigid. Have you dug a shelter beside an Undying tree where you will take all your wives and children and hide deep inside until the war passes? Will they use the red clay of the shelter's wall to make themselves beautiful for you while you pass the time speaking natural mathematics to the Seven? Big man you are now with your beard and apprentice status."

"You mock your own people now," he said.

"I'm trying to *save* it!"

"If you hadn't left in the first place, this wouldn't be happening," he snapped.

"I *had* to leave," I said. "Dele, I'm not . . . I'm not meant to stay here. You know it. You've always known it. I was always going out into the desert. You know? Because it's huge, it's vast. When I look back, the desert and space, they feel similar."

"Well, *I* was always meant to go inward, into what makes us *us*," he said. "And that's just as vast. And doing that will make me the next chief, not get us destroyed."

His words were like a punch in the chest and suddenly I felt breathless. War was coming as we stood here arguing. Who knew what Mwinyi and Okwu were saying to the elders. And the one who knew me even before I was fully me harbored such a dislike of me that it seemed he would have been happier if I'd died on the Third Fish last year.

"Let me do my part to fix this, Dele," I begged him. "The elders can convince the Khoush to come. I know how to call the Meduse to come. Then, the Himba Council can use Himba deep culture to get them to make peace with the Meduse."

Dele seemed to think about this, walking away from me toward the Sacred Well. He leaned against the stone wellhead and looked down into it. He turned to me. "You can call them? How?"

I didn't look away. I was what I was and I was many things now. I touched my *okuoko*. "With these."

"Your hair?"

"They're not hair anymore."

"So it's true," he said. "You've become the wife of a Meduse."

I frowned. "I'm no one's wife."

"You came home and you came with it," he said. "It stayed at the home of your family. It's been intimate with you enough that your body has changed."

"Okwu didn't do this," I said. "I don't even know which of—"

"The Meduse are a hive-minded people," he said. "What one does, they all do. If you use those to communicate with Okwu, you're communicating with the others, too."

"No," I said. "Only Okwu. And in a distant way, the Meduse chief. You don't understand."

"I've heard some of the story of what you went through from your father. Okwu would have killed you on that ship, but on Oomza University, it's your closest companion. You've become Okwu's wife."

I dismissively waved a hand at him. "Just help me, Dele. Just go talk to them. They'll hear you."

"Did you really see the Night Masquerade?"

I nodded.

"Twice?"

I nodded again. "Second time was on the road outside the Root."

"Earlier today?"

"Yes."

"During the day?"

"Yes."

"Unbelievable. *Kai!*" he exclaimed, striding away from me. Then he stopped and came back.

"What?" I softly asked as he walked up to me. I flinched as he reached forward and took one of my *okuoko* and lightly pressed it. My hand shot out before I realized I was going to do it and slapped his hand away. "Stop!" I said.

He looked at the *otjize* on his hand and then at my *okuoko,* whose transparent blue now showed a bit. He sniffed my *otjize* and then gazed at me for several moments. He eyed me as he rubbed his short beard with the *otjize* on his fingers, then he turned and walked away.

I stepped over to the wellhead and looked down into the water. Down into the darkness that was nothing like the darkness of space. Not as complete. Not as foreign. When I heard shouting and then rumbling loud enough to shake the building, I turned and strode outside. "No, no, no, no!" I muttered. We'd run out of time.

The Khoush sky whales, each the size of two houses, landed in the desert, close enough to whip dust into the air that nearly put out the Sacred Fire. The Khoush knew exactly where they were landing. The Khoush had no respect for my people. Each ship was covered with blue and white solar tiles with giant wind turbines under each wing. They'd always reminded me of beetles with the skin of lizards.

And though they moved smoothly through the sky like water beetles in water, they landed in such a way that everyone in the area would know it.

As two of the elders scrambled to stand before the fire and hold open their garments to protect it, Dele, Chief Kapika, and Titi gathered together to meet whoever alighted from the sky whales. I ran to Okwu and Mwinyi.

Okwu, hide! I shouted through my *okuoko*. It turned to me. *You should—*

Okwu flew at me just as I heard a sharp *zip!* Then Okwu's *okuoko* and then its dome was covering me. I felt every part of my body tense up. There was weight but not much, but also a sense of being enveloped and gently held, hugged. Protected. Okwu's flesh smelled like pepper seed, spicy and hot. I could see everything right through it, tinted a blue. Chief Kapika and Dele were running at the sky whales, waving their hands, shouting, putting themselves in the space between Okwu, Mwinyi, and me and the sky whales. Then Okwu was releasing its gas all around us and the shocked look of Mwinyi, the laboring smoky fire, and a few of the elders who'd turned our way disappeared. I instinctively held my breath.

Seconds passed and I leaned back, my own *okuoko* writhing on my head. I could feel the vibration of Okwu's body and then a hardness against my arm. Its stinger. White and sharp. And a thought came to me heavy with relief. If Okwu was protecting me, then it was not killing Khoush. I felt Okwu shudder and I was expelled. I tumbled onto the sand and without looking at myself, I knew most of my *otjize* had been sucked off. The night air felt cool on my bare flesh.

I looked back at Okwu and saw that several of its *okuoko* were hanging by a thread or shot off, its blue color looking lighter in the firelight. Maybe pink. *Red?* I wondered. Then I was sure. Okwu was spattered with blood. *My blood?* I thought, but I didn't look at myself because Okwu lowered to the ground. I'd never seen a Meduse touch the ground. "Okwu!" I exclaimed, scrambling to it on my knees. Okwu now lay to the side, like a deflated balloon. I gently touched its dome, tears squeezing from my eyes, barely able to breathe. Okwu's dome felt tough like the bladders of water that women carried to and from the lake. Cool beneath my touch. "What's the matter?" I shouted. "*What's the matter?*"

"They shot it," Mwinyi was saying as he came and knelt beside me.

"Why didn't you use your shield?" I asked.

"You'd . . . have . . . died if I did," it said, its voice deeper and rougher than ever. It made my head hurt.

Mwinyi placed a hand on Okwu's dome as he stared intensely at it. Okwu's flesh twitched at his touch, but then calmed. I looked behind us and gasped. There had to be at least a hundred Khoush soldiers; men and women standing stiffly in tight desert pants and tops, the women in black and the men in white. Two Khoush men and one Khoush woman, all also in army gear, stood speaking with

Chief Kapika, Titi, and Dele, the others standing eagerly behind them.

"It is in pain," Mwinyi said. "It won't speak to me."

I couldn't think. Mama, Papa, my siblings, family dead. Zinariya crippling me. The Night Masquerade's ominous appearance. War was here. I could barely take in enough breath to keep from passing out. My heart felt as if it would burst through my chest. *Heru's chest burst open and his blood on my face was warm.* I wanted to throw myself over Okwu and scream and wail. Submit. I looked at Okwu, then back at the Khoush and the elders, then back at Okwu. I frowned, reaching into my pocket and touching the gold ball. My hand brushed against my jar of *otjize*. I was about to let myself tree for clarity. Then to myself, I said, "No."

Mwinyi looked at me questioningly.

I grabbed the jar of *otjize* in my pocket. Okwu's insides were slathered with a lot of it already. "Mwinyi, put this where Okwu's been injured," I said. I paused and then added, "Use all of it."

I stood up.

As I walked toward them all, they could have shot me. They'd just tried. I was too angry to care. The Khoush soldiers stood like statues as I approached. In rows, before their sky whales, the darkness of the desert extending behind them, the stars above. My sandals dug into the sand. My red skirt lapped at my legs and my red top was wet with sweat. No *otjize*. I was naked.

"Binti," one of the Khoush men said.

"I don't know who you are," I said, standing beside Dele. He was staring at me like I was a creature from outer space. All of them were.

"Qalb Leader Iyad," he said. "And these are my co-leaders, Qalb Leader Durrah." The tall woman with the thin braid hanging to her knees nodded at me. "And Qalb Leader Yabani." The intense-looking man with an equally long black braid inhaled noisily, flaring his nostrils at me as if he'd smelled something foul. All of them had light brown skin, darkened from its typical Khoush tone by the sun.

"We've told them of your suggestion," Chief Kapika quickly said. "That you offer to convince the Meduse to attend a meeting to make peace." He gave me a slight nod and I felt a rush of relief, despite all that had just happened. The Himba Council would be there too.

"We will take the idea to General Kuw and he will take it to the king of Khoushland," Iyad said, looking down his nose at me. "But the Meduse massacred a ship full of our most gifted minds, unarmed students and professors. And all that was left was . . . you. Can you really convince those savages to come and have a rational discussion?"

I don't know when I started shaking, but when I spoke, my voice was vibrating like an Undying tree during a thunderstorm. "You just tried to kill me," I blurted.

Yabani laughed.

"That was an accident," Iyad said. "We thought you were a Meduse."

I felt Dele try to take my arm. "Breathe," he said into my ear.

I yanked my arm away. I could feel my *okuoko* writhing wildly now. Without *otjize* what must I have looked like? "You shot my friend," I growled. "It's the third time you people have tried to kill it since we arrived here! You agreed to the pact through Oomza Uni knowing you were lying right through your teeth."

"I doubt one dead Meduse is a pact destroyer after they killed a ship full of our smartest and finest," Iyad snapped. "They're barely flesh, anyway."

My vision blurred with fury. "Khoush scholars attacked the Meduse chief, took its stinger, and put it on display in a museum!" I stepped right up to Iyad's face. I am not tall. Nor am I roped with muscle. I barely came to this man's chin and I had to look up to meet his eyes, but he was scared. I saw it in his face. I smelled it wafting from his naked skin. He was terrified of me. I'd seen the Night Masquerade twice, I was Meduse, I was Enyi Zinariya, I was Himba, and I had no home.

"I am Binti Ekeopara Zuzu Dambu Kaipka Meduse Enyi Zinariya of Osemba, master harmonizer," I said. I let myself tree and though I felt calmer, my rage stayed and I was glad. I called up a current and held up my hands to show it connecting to my index fingers like soft lightning. I swirled my fingers and the current coiled into a ball hovering before Iyad's eyes. "I do not want to see my homeland and people destroyed by a stale ancient irrational fight between people who have no real reason to hate each other. When the sun rises, come as you've agreed, to the Root that you reduced to char and ash, where my family lies dead. The Meduse *will* be there and you both will bury this idiocy once and for all." *With the help and power of us Himba,* I thought, angrily. *Because neither of you is reasonable enough to do it on your own.*

I didn't wait for his answer. I pulled in my current, turned, and walked back to Okwu and Mwinyi.

~

The Khoush left. I didn't see them go, but I heard their sky whales take off and felt the dust they blew over us.

Okwu did not die. My *otjize* saved him. Both the *otjize* Mwinyi slathered on its wounds and the *otjize* Okwu had sucked off my skin and *okuoko* when it had enveloped me. Mwinyi, his fingers coated with what was left of my *otjize,* wouldn't stop looking at me.

That night, we stayed in the Osemba House. Somehow, we'd been able to fit Okwu through the dome-shaped door that was wide but not nearly as wide as Okwu. The Meduse were huge but easily compressible, when they wanted to be. Iyad had been rude in his words, but correct, nonetheless. There really *wasn't* much mass or weight to Meduse. Once inside, Okwu hovered weakly beside the well. It was quiet, glad to be near such pure water, its god. Mwinyi took a bucket of it out back and bathed with it.

I can't say that I didn't have the urge to do the same, and this disturbed me.

The elders and Dele could not deal with me being *otjize*-free. Thus, after Titi and the other women brought us food and blankets and promised to check on our camel, they left us. They would meet us in the morning. Out back, the Sacred Fire burned, small now and fueled by the bark of an Undying tree, so it would not go out, as long as no sky whale wind turbines blew dust on it. Titi brought me a jar of *otjize* and now I sat on a blanket facing the back door and Sacred Fire, contemplating the large jar on the mat before my crossed legs.

Mwinyi sat beside me and picked up the jar. I let him open it and sniff the contents. "This one and the other I put on Okwu smells different from your own," he said.

I smiled. "Mine was made from clay I dug up on Oomza Uni."

He put the jar back down and turned to me. "Is it an insult if I said you look beautiful with it *and* without it?"

I met his eyes for only a moment and then looked away, my heart fluttering.

"I can see you more clearly now," he said. "Now that I've seen you with it and without. The two make one."

"You're not supposed to *ever* see me without *otjize,*" I said. "Only a Himba girl's parents should ever see a Himba girl my age without her *otjize*. Not even a woman's husband will—" I bit my lip and looked at the jar.

"I know," Mwinyi laughed. "But remember, I'm not Himba. Me seeing you with and without it just means I see you. Nothing demeaning." He touched the long matted braid that grew from the middle of his red-brown bushy hair. It was so long that it reached his knees. "See this? The Enyi Zinariya call it *tsani,* a 'ladder' for the spirits. You start growing it at the age of ten. So it's been seven years. A woman isn't supposed to touch it and not even my mother has." He hesitated for a moment and then held it out to me.

I looked at it. "Are you sure?" I asked. "Why?"

"Do you know the desert dogs we met didn't think you were from Earth?" he said. "I think, maybe, I think you're part of something, Binti." His confident smile was faltering now. This was anything but easy for him. I looked at the rope of red-brown hair. Then I reached out and took it in my hands. It felt like my hair, except it wasn't made firm with *otjize*.

"There," I said, putting it down. "Do you feel different?"

"No," he said. "But I am." He smirked and then laughed.

"What's funny?" I asked.

He grinned bigger than I'd seen him grin since we'd left his home. "Honestly, I'm not even sure if you're a human being anymore, so maybe you don't really count."

I laughed, gently shoving him away. We sat there for a moment, gazing at the Sacred Fire. I could feel the darkness of my family's death trying to pull me down, and I scooted closer to Mwinyi. He turned to me and touched my *okuoko* and I didn't push his hand away.

"You shouldn't allow that, Binti," Okwu said from behind us.

Mwinyi quickly let go and stood up. Then he knelt back down, brought his face to mine, and kissed me. When he pulled back, we looked into each other's eyes smiling and . . .

Then darkness.

Then I was there again . . .

. . . I was in space. Infinite blackness. Weightless. Flying, falling, ascending, traveling, through a planet's ring of brittle metallic dust. It pelted my flesh like chips of glittery ice. I opened my mouth a bit to breathe, the dust hitting my lips. Could I breathe?

Living breath bloomed in my chest from within me and I felt my lungs expand, filling with it. I relaxed.

"Who are you?" a voice asked. It spoke in Otjihimba and it came and it came from everywhere.

"Binti Ekeopara Zuzu Dambu Kaipka of Namib, that is my name," I said.

Pause.

"There's more," the voice said.

"That's all," I said, irritated. "That's my name."

"No."

This was true but the truth of it made me flinch . . .

. . . I fell out of the tree. From Mwinyi's eyes. My gold ball was floating beside us. Rotating like a small planet. It dropped to my mat.

"Where did you go?" he asked, leaning away from me. "Where was that?"

"You saw it too?"

"It's different when it's human master harmonizers," Okwu said from behind us.

"I know that place," Mwinyi said. "That's the ring of Saturn."

I frowned, "How do you know? I thought you said you'd never left Earth."

"I haven't, but the Zinariya have," he said. "And they gave us the zinariya. I've looked at their memories of space travel; Saturn and Jupiter have always been my favorites. Why are you seeing Saturn's ring? Flying through it like a bird?"

"It's something the *edan* keeps showing me," I said. "Even after it fell apart. Maybe I'm meant to go there."

"Never seen a Himba constantly called to leave home," Mwinyi said more to himself than me. He kissed me again, and this time I leaned forward and took his face in my hands and kissed him back. He wrapped his arms around me and pulled me close and for a while, we lost ourselves in each other. Dele and I had shared kisses a few times when we were younger, but his strong traditional beliefs made him begin to keep his distance as we grew older. And when my friend Eba had asked me to sneak away with her behind the bushes as some of the girls liked to do, I had laughed and said, "No thank you."

Now, I was overwhelmed. There were no taboos or hesitations in the way. And when I pulled my lips from Mwinyi's, his arms still around me, I didn't look into his eyes. "I feel like I'm falling," I breathed. He kissed me one more time and let go. I was leaning on my elbows on the mat, my body throbbing and my mind a swirl of so much, when he stood up.

"I need to go into the desert," he said. "I'll be back." I held up a hand and he took it. "You should remove your sandals and stand outside in the sand," he added. "It'll ground you and that way, you won't feel so much like you're falling. Because you're not."

"That's what the Night Masquerade said to me."

"It spoke?"

I hesitated then nodded. "It said, 'Death is always news. A bird who has flown off the earth and then returns to land is still on the land. Remove your shoes and listen.' "

Mwinyi clucked his tongue as he wrapped his braid around his finger. "I repeat, maybe you should take your sandals off and go stand outside," he said.

I went back to looking at the jar of *otjize* after he left. I picked it up and put it back down. I sighed, unsure. I picked it up and stood up. "Okwu, are you alright?" I said.

"I would tell you if I were not," it said, puffing out enough gas to envelope itself.

I coughed. "I'm going to stand outside near the fire for a bit."

"I will be here listening to the waters below," Okwu said.

The night was cool, but the fire made the area around it warm, even at its decreased size. Its light reached out into the open desert, but where it did not reach was blackness.

It reminded me of when I looked out the window while traveling in the Third Fish. Though that blankness was much deeper.

I put the *otjize* beside me and raised my hands. "*Are you alright?*" I typed. Then I pushed the red words off into the desert. They fled as if blown by a powerful invisible wind, scaling and disappearing over a nearby sand dune in the direction Mwinyi had gone. A moment later, "*Yes. Get some rest. Don't test the zinariya,*" came back to me in his green letters. Then I heard the strange whispers and it seemed as if I saw a planet peeking over the horizon. I looked down, closing my eyes until the whispering stopped. When I opened them, the planet was gone.

Despite Mwinyi's warning, I considered testing my tolerance of distant zinariya. I needed to reach my grandmother and tell her what happened. It needed to be me, not Mwinyi. But if I tried and my still fresh mind reacted badly to the attempt again, with Mwinyi gone I only had the injured Okwu to help me. Okwu needed rest. *No,* I thought. *I'll tell my grandmother when I have some good news. I'll try after sunrise.* Another sunrise in a world where my family was dead. I felt the hot embers in my chest begin to burn. Quickly pushing the pain away, I thought to Okwu, *Can you hear me?* My *okuoko* wriggled gently on the sides of my face and against my shoulders. He was close, so my effort did not have to be much.

Yes.

I sighed, bringing the golden ball from my pocket. I no

longer thought of it as an *edan;* I saw it more like a little planet. No reason. It was just what was. And I was floating around it, untethered, homeless. I allowed myself to tree and then called up and ran a current over it and watched it rise before my eyes on the electric blue current, slowly rotating. I reached up and took it in my hands, running the pads of my fingers over its fingerprint-like surface.

I picked up the jar of *otjize,* unscrewed the lid, and dug my index and middle fingers into it. I spread it on my body.

Chapter 4

Homecoming

The first class I took at Oomza Uni was Treeing 101. It started the equivalent of seven Earth days after I'd reached Oomza Uni alive and become a hero. It was one of several first-year student classes from all specialties—from Weapons to Math to Organics to Travel, and more. I placed out of it that first day. The class was conducted in one of the large fields between Math, Weapons, and Organics Cities. The dry yellow grasses there had been cut low but still were occupied by hopping ntu ntu bugs, their brilliant orange-pink pigmentation eye-catching in the sunlight. All the students sat in a huge circle to listen to the instructor Professor Osisi, who looked like a tall wide tree with fanlike leaves bigger than my head.

We were all dazzled as Professor Osisi called up ten thick currents at once *as* it told us about the class. After what felt like a half-hour of talking (I was still adjusting to the faster cycle on Oomza Uni), we were split into smaller groups of about six, in which teaching assistants had us each step forward and tree in front of our groups. In my group were two Meduse-like people, someone who looked like a crab made of diamonds, and three blue humanoid types who kept touching my *okuoko* and humming in a way that seemed a lot like laughter to me. None of us spoke similar languages, though all of us spoke in sound.

"My name is Assistant Sagar," our teacher said, a sleek hairless foxlike person with eyes on its snout who stood on two legs at my height. When it spoke, it touched something near its throat and though I understood it, I also heard other voices speaking at the same time, probably in languages the others could understand. I smiled, delighted. The way people on Oomza Uni were so diverse and everyone handled that as if it were normal continued to surprise me. It was so unlike Earth, where wars were fought over and because of differences and most couldn't relate to anyone unless they were similar.

"This is a placement test," Sagar said. "You will step up and face the group and tree as well as you can."

"What if we can't really do it well?" the one who looked like a giant crab made of diamonds asked. It was beside me and clearly agitated as each of its legs kept stamping on the grass, sending ntu ntu bugs leaping this way and that. I grinned again. I could understand it, too! Whatever Sagar was using to communicate with all of us, it connected our group as well. I turned to the group closest to me, which was a few feet away; all I heard were grunts, humming, and a "pop pop pop."

Not one individual in my group could tree with difficulty, let alone with ease. When I took my turn, Sagar said,

"Good. At least there's one. And you might be the only one in the entire class today." I was. In a class of over two hundred new students, I was the only one who could tree. This would not have been the case if all the other students on my ship hadn't been wiped out; Heru could tree as well as I could. This added to the other reasons students mostly kept their distance from me. In that group, where we'd all stayed close to each other as we each waited to be tested, as soon as I got up there, did what I could do, and then moved aside for someone else to try, I knew I was apart again.

After the last two students took their turns, I looked at the sky above. I'd once read about a phenomenon that happened in the colder parts of Earth when oxygen and nitrogen in the atmosphere collided with electrically charged particles released from the sun. The resulting swirls of green lights were beautiful and strange and though I never wanted to go to a part of Earth where there was snow and intense cold, I'd been curious what these lights would look like. As I stood away from my fellow students I realized that, with so many trying to descend into mathematical trance and call up current, the air had charged. The odd pinkish orange bright sky swirled with green-blue lights. I could even feel the charged air on my skin. I'd stood there for minutes looking up and reveling in the feeling of so much possibility and newness.

Now, in the Osemba House, I awoke feeling like I did that day on Oomza Uni—the hairs on my hands standing on end, the feeling of energy all around me. I opened my eyes and sat straight up. Mwinyi was nearby on his mat and he stirred but didn't awaken. Then I heard it, a rumble from far away and a low haunted howling.

I got up and walked out the back door. Okwu was already there, floating easily before the fire. Its *okuoko* that were intact looked fully healed and the ones that had hanging tips were shorter, the tips having fallen off. But at least they were blue again.

"I thought you didn't like the fire," I said.

"I've grown used to it now."

Warm wind blew off the desert and from afar I could see a flash of lightning.

"It's still far," Okwu said.

"But it's coming," I said. "It doesn't rain much here. But I hope it'll arrive after sunrise." I paused and then asked, "Will your chief agree to a truce?"

Okwu didn't answer for a long time and I began to wish I hadn't asked.

"Meduse aren't the problem," Okwu finally said. "Your council must succeed. And I think you need to be careful."

~

We left the Osemba House with about an hour until dawn. It was windy and the overcast sky made it even darker, and thus easier to see the occasional flash of lightning in the distance. I shut the door behind me and when I turned, I was shocked that I actually had a reason to smile.

"Oh!" I exclaimed as we left the Osemba House. "You're glowing."

Okwu, who'd regained most of its strength, vibrated its dome. "I took from your lake," it said. "Those snails."

"The clusterwinks?" I asked, gently touching its softly glowing blue dome. The bioluminescent snails lived in the lake and happened to be spawning when we arrived. Okwu had been covered with them when it had emerged from the lake yesterday.

"Yes," it said. "When Meduse spend a lot of time with such things, we absorb their genetic coding and make it our own."

"Is Binti going to start glowing too?" Mwinyi asked. I frowned at him as he snickered.

Okwu's dome vibrated, but it said nothing.

Okwu's glow came in handy. The overcast sky, blowing dust, and the Osemba-wide blackout left the streets darker than normal. With my astrolabe broken, I had nothing to help light the way. Even the glow from bioluminescent flowers on some of the homes and buildings was muted. We walked close to each other, this time completely alone and unwatched as we journeyed across Osemba back to the Root.

With each step I took through my hometown, I wondered what I was walking toward, purposely bringing myself closer to. I'd needed to reconnect with my family after I'd left the way I did and with all that went on to happen, but realistically, it was my own insecurities that brought me running home so soon. When the Meduse anger had come forth, I'd immediately assumed something was wrong with me instead of realizing that it was simply a new change to which I had to adjust. I'd thought something was wrong with me because my family thought something was wrong with me. And now my childish actions had brought death and war. What had I started? Whatever it was, I had to finish it.

The wind blew harder and I was glad for the layer of *otjize* I'd put on my skin and rolled over my *okuoko.* As we passed the group of Undying trees, Mwinyi and I pressed our hands to our ears and Okwu rushed up the road so fast that I lost sight of it. Mwinyi and I stopped, completely in the dark.

"Okwu!" I called. But the noise drowned out my voice. I called it through my *okuoko.* Far up the road between two homes, it stopped.

Just come, I heard it say in my mind. *I cannot be near those evil trees.*

I looked at Mwinyi.

"I have an idea," I quickly said, trying not to look at the trees yards away that were vibrating so fast that they looked like a blur. I relaxed as I focused on the powerful gusty wind and raised my hands and typed through the zinariya as I spoke the words. The equation "w = ½ r A v3" floated in red before me, then it began to blow toward Okwu like a flag attached to an invisible pole in front of me. As I watched it, I raised my hands and called up a bright ball of current.

The dusty road, vibrating trees, the storefront across the street, and the people looking out the window from the home beside it were all illuminated by my light. Mwinyi and I took one look at the Undying trees and quickly moved on. Even when we caught up to Okwu, I continued to use my light. And in this way, as we reached the part of Osemba near my home where the Khoush had taken out their anger when they couldn't find Okwu and me, we saw that several of the half-destroyed homes had caved in or toppled because of the wind. This last block of homes and buildings looked like the old images of Khoushland cities and towns during the Khoush-Meduse wars decades ago. Pockmarked walls, blasted homes, crumbled buildings. Sandstone wasn't made to survive war, and stone buildings, like the Root, could be exploded to rubble and even burned.

Treeing helped me clear my mind of worry and the strong light gave me what felt like my last view of Osemba.

~

The Root had stopped burning.

Now it was just a mound of char, much of the ash blown into the desert by the winds of the coming storm. Sunrise was close and all I could do was stand before the mound and stare. The only person who met us at the Root when we arrived was our camel Rakumi, who had, indeed, eaten all that remained of my brother's garden. The Himba Council had promised to meet us here but it was nowhere in sight. Not even Dele.

"They're just late," I said.

Minutes passed and there still wasn't a sign of them. So to add to my despair and worry, I looked at my home. The wind had blown so much away and revealed the remains—a black foundation of charred wood. The opening to the cellar must have been burned shut. Still holding the ball of current, my mind numb and empty, I stared and stared.

Across what was left of my home, I could see Okwu inspecting the remains of the tent my father had made it—which was nothing but a cracking mess formed from sand heated so hot by the explosion of Khoush weapons that it had become a yellow-black glass. Mwinyi was digging and knocking at the char at the base of the Root's foundation.

"What are you doing?" I called.

"Looking," he distractedly said, pressing both his hands to it now.

I clucked my tongue, irritated. What if he caused the entire thing to cave in? What would he reveal? I shivered. "Mwinyi!" I called. "Please stop doing—"

The thunder rumbled, this time louder, and it was blended with a deeper, more urgent purring. "Oh no," I whispered. Slowly, I turned to the west, dust spraying squarely in my face. The Khoush were here. From Kokure in Khoushland? Further west? The skyline seemed to be crowded with sky whales. They flew smoothly, despite the high winds and charged air.

I spat out dust and blinked my eyes as Okwu joined me, positioning itself in front of me. "No," I said, stepping aside. "This is for peace. If they shoot me, then—"

"You will be dead," Okwu said, getting in front of me.

"Don't be a fool, Binti," Mwinyi said, joining us. He too moved in front of me. "If the Himba Council isn't here . . ." He bit his lip. "Maybe they set us up."

When the ships landed, the number of soldiers that poured out and the sheer amount of artillery that they unpacked was incredible. Within minutes, the expanse of desert was occupied with hundreds of waiting Khoush soldiers standing in formation, several of the sky whales had broken down into weaponized land shuttles, and there were long sticks with black hoops that extended into the sky whose function I didn't know.

"I thought they'd just bring an envoy," I muttered as three Khoush walked up to us.

"They have always been about show," Okwu rumbled in Meduse.

"Translation, please," Mwinyi said.

"They like to show power," I told him in Otjihimba. "Okwu, shall I call them now?"

"You said sunrise," Okwu said. "They will come."

And sure enough, as the sun peeked over the horizon, before the three Khoush members got to us, they stopped and looked toward Osemba. I turned as well. The Meduse ships looked like they belonged in the water. Bulbous and glowing a deep purple blue, they looked like larger versions of the Meduse themselves. I briefly wondered if they were, for I'd been inside one a year ago and it had felt like being inside the body of a living thing, and stunk like one too. They silently landed, the ships' *okuoko* whipped about and their bodies buffeted gently by the winds.

Chapter 5

Homegoing

I stood between the leaders of both sides.

I could barely look at Goldie, the Khoush's king. I'd only seen his face on the news feeds and heard the Khoush who came into my father's shop speak of him as the Honorable One. He was a tall stout man with pale skin that looked as if it never saw the sun. His garments were immaculately white, glowing and blowing in the dusty wind.

Flanking his left and right were his military commanders whom he'd introduced as his minister of defense, a plump tan-skinned woman named Lady who had severe eyes, and Commander of General Staff Kuw, a muscle-bound man with a shiny bald head who looked only a few years my senior. I recognized Kuw's name. He was the one Okwu said had set the Root on fire. Even from where I stood, I could feel Okwu's hatred for especially Kuw.

Scuttling behind them was the Khoush mayor of Kokure, Alhaji Truck Omaze. He nodded at me, flashing the same smile as when I'd stepped off the Third Fish days ago. Had he known of the plan to assassinate Okwu even back then at the launch port when things had so nearly gone wrong?

If not at that point, he probably knew soon after we left for Osemba. I scowled back at him.

The Meduse chief came with two of its military heads, first-in-command Mbu and its second-in-command, named Nke Abuo. Unlike the clear-fleshed chief, Mbu and Nke Abuo looked blue and opaque like Okwu. Okwu stood between me and the Khoush.

I looked at both groups. Each seemed to be waiting for me to speak. I wanted to crawl into myself. I felt small. I opened my mouth and closed it. The Khoush king was looking at me like I was something useless. I glanced at the Meduse chief, whom I'd last seen while on a different planet, after I had saved everyone, after I'd been so brave. This was Earth, where I was just a Himba girl.

"The Himba Council haven't arrived yet," Mwinyi said, stepping up beside me.

"We're not going to wait much longer," King Goldie said, giving the Meduse chief a hard look.

"Neither will we," the chief rumbled in Meduse.

"It said, 'Neither will we,' " Okwu translated to Mwinyi.

We were all quiet. I glanced at the mound of char; Meduse rage and indignation flooded into me so suddenly that I twitched. The Khoush king was right here, before me. I spoke. "Do you know who I am?"

Goldie smirked and I felt angrier. "Of course I do. You're more dignified and well-spoken than I expected." He chuckled. "And at least I can hear you clearly. Himba women and girls are so soft-spoken."

"Do you know what that mound is?" I asked.

Above, thunder rumbled and I felt even stronger. Before he responded, I let myself tree. My mind cleared and I thanked the Seven for that because of what King Goldie of the Khoush said next.

"Your family harbored the enemy," he said, his smirk dropping completely. "They suffered the consequences." He motioned to where the Root had been. "If it were up to me, that would be a hole in the ground. "

I felt my *okuoko* begin to writhe on my head and slap at my neck and back, but I held steady, equations circulating around my head. The golden ball in my pocket was warm and rotating. I took a deep, deep breath, imagining the air filling my toes all the way up my body as my therapist had taught me. Then, as she also taught me, I stepped back from all of them, looking every single one of them in the eye, ending with Goldie. But Goldie didn't even notice.

He turned to his commander of general staff and said, "The Himba are a cowardly people."

Kuw nodded. "They hide when they get scared. Like intelligent, innovative desert foxes."

I opened my mouth to speak, but then closed it. I pressed my lips shut, shaking with anger as I looked around. Where *was* the council? I met Mwinyi's eyes and he mouthed, "Just wait. They'll come." But every second was sending the plan closer to failure. Above, the storm churned in the sky, the thunder crashing now, lightning flashing. I called up a current to calm myself and let it linger around each of my hands. The feeling of the current and the way it drew from the lightning above without drawing the lightning down made me feel powerful. I stood up straighter.

"I will not speak to the Khoush," the Meduse chief said to Okwu. "This is not how we agreed things would go." Then to me, it said, "Binti, where are the men of your council?"

Goldie had completely turned his back on me to speak with his commander and minister of defense. "I only gave this a chance because of my relationship to the president of Oomza Uni. A meeting of men and instead, only this foolish Himba girl is here. We should—"

It was the phrase "foolish Himba girl." That's what did it. In that phrase was condescension, a mockery of my high standing at Oomza Uni, a spitting on my family and the Himba as a whole. And where *was* the council? I didn't care. My family was dead. Everyone kept dying in the ship. I saw Heru's chest burst open again and I felt my *okuoko* writhing as every part of my being filled with rage. Doors deep within me flew open. All of them. All at the same time. My body waved forward, then backward, as I felt the current I was holding expand. Lightning flashed above and something in me decided to do something I'd never done: grab it.

I fell out of the tree. Then *POW!* the current I'd drawn poured into me.

I awoke. I knew something very, very important. I knew that everything depended on that moment. I wasn't sure exactly how, but the destiny of my people was temporarily in my hands.

And so, I screamed, *"I'm the one who called this meeting! This was my idea!"* I faced King Goldie, my eyes wide and wild. He'd whirled around, gawking at me now. Current surrounded me in an electric blue spiral that felt warm on my skin and protective. At the same time, I spoke these words through my *okuoko* to the Meduse chief in my roughest Meduse. My hands moved as if owned by a part of myself that had its own intent and soon I was pushing those same words into the desert. When I did this, my world remained as it was . . . because it was already expanded.

The words returned to me as if whispered from afar. Not in text, but in sound. "You tell them, Binti." It was my grandmother's voice. With my peripheral vision, I saw Mwinyi suddenly turn and run toward the Root.

"I'm not crazy," I said, addressing all. I faced King Goldie as I spoke. "I'm *not* small. I'm *not* foolish." I paused for a moment. "Do any of you even remember why you started fighting? The Meduse tried to drain the lakes? The Khoush massacred a tribe of peaceful Meduse explorers? The Khoushland chief's daughter was kidnapped? If I ask each of you the reason, you'll cite different stories from so long ago that the grandchildren of the grandchildren of any possible witnesses are long dead." I turned to the chief. "What do you want with these lands? Your god is water, maybe there was water when this war began, but this part of the Earth is parched of it now. In my town, the trees had to tell us where to find water so we wouldn't die. Khoushland is mostly desert, while seventy-one percent of the Earth is water! Why not go there? There aren't many humans who live on the oceans. You can frolic in those waters with no trouble. But you'd rather fight and die and kill for a drop of water in a dry land."

I turned to Goldie. "And you Khoush, who *don't* you look down upon? The Himba create technology that allows your whole community to thrive and you repay us by behaving as if we're your slaves. Because what? What makes Khoush superior to Himba? Tell me! Then your egos are bruised when one of us befriends and brings a Meduse as a show of peace. So you try to assassinate it, knowing that it's one of the ultimate forms of disrespect to the Himba, knowing that this will bring war from the Meduse! You took their chief's stinger, just to show you had the power to do it, and you complain when they retaliate."

I took a deep breath.

"I incite the deep culture of the Himba." I looked intensely at both King Goldie and the Meduse chief. "Neither of you know of it and that is okay. The Himba Council members were to do this, but I think they're afraid. I think they're hiding. I'm not. And I'm a collective within myself, so I can.

"Meduse tradition is one of honor. Khoush tradition is one of respect. I am master harmonizer of the Osemba

Himba." I raised my hands, the currents swirling into balls in both hands like blue suns. I held one toward Goldie. "The one who represents the Khoush." I held a hand toward the Meduse chief. "The one who represents the Meduse." I steadied myself. I pulled from deep within me, from the earth beneath my feet, from what I could reach beyond the Earth above. Because I was a master harmonizer and my path was through mathematics, I took what came and felt it as numbers, absorbed it as math, and when I spoke, I breathed it out. "Please," I said, the words coming from my mouth cool in my throat, pouring over my tongue and lips. I was doing it; I was speaking the words to power. I was uttering deep culture. "End this," I said, my voice full and steady. "End this now."

As soon as the words had left my lips, my throat began to burn. Lightning flashed, immediately followed by the crash of thunder. The noise didn't shake me, the threat of lightning would never scare me again. I felt it still within me, though it was dissipating now. From my feet and through the top of my head, through the tips of my writhing *okuoko*. I felt as if I were both sinking and levitating. Draining and spouting. That is the deep culture. Never in a thousand years would I have believed it would move through *me*. Never. *If Dele were here to see, he would be on his knees in amazement,* I thought. But he wasn't. None of the council was here.

"Okay, Binti," Goldie said, his voice soft and his face slack with awe as he gazed at me. He nodded. "I . . . I agree to the truce."

The Meduse chief breathed out a great puff of its gas and so did his two comrades and Okwu. Several of the Meduse hovering near the ship did the same. Then the chief spoke to me in Meduse. "I will listen to the Binti. She is right. This fight is useless."

"The war between Khoush and Meduse ends," I said, bringing my hands together. Immediately, both balls of current extinguished, sending a ripple of energy through me that made me stumble back as it all stopped. I coughed, tasting blood in my mouth. Above, the storm having blown itself out, the sky began to clear, sunrise's light.

I smiled as the Khoush king and Meduse chief both went back to their people.

"Well done," Okwu said in Otjihimba.

I nodded to him. It was so quiet now, the wind having died down to a strong breeze and the lightning and its thunder retreating into the sky. I looked around for Mwinyi and didn't quickly see him. I looked up at the sky, a large sliver of sun shining through the dissipating clouds.

"Thank the Seven," I said, my voice rough. "Thank Them for giving me all I needed to do it." I laughed.

When I brought my gaze back down, my eyes fell on a very strange sight. For the third time, I was seeing it: the Night Masquerade. Again, during the day. It stood on the dirt road that led to my home. The road I'd walked down when I'd left home in the dark of early morning. No smoke billowed from its head this time. In the silence, I could hear its drumbeat as it danced, kicking up dust as it shook its raffia hips and raised its long arms. I knew only one person who danced like that.

"Dele?" I whispered, squinting.

I jumped when I heard the shots. At first, I was so focused on the Night Masquerade that I thought they were sharp drumbeats. Then I felt a powerful zap in my *okuoko* as vibration shivered into my forehand, face, and neck. My eyes watered with the pain and when I turned toward the Meduse ships, I saw a ball of fire smash into the Meduse chief.

I didn't hear Meduse voices in my head, I heard a collective shriek. Then I knew it more than saw it, for the armor Okwu had created on Oomza Uni was clear and fit over its body perfectly. Every single Meduse, outside and on their ships, was encased in this armor. Including the chief, who floated back upright, flanked by two of its commanders. Then the Meduse ship began smoothly flying into a battle formation, its movements rippling and fluid like water . . . this was army-scale *moojh-ha ki-bira*. I turned to the Khoush just in time to see one of their sky whale ships explode. More Khoush soldiers on the ground fled.

A rough hand grabbed my right arm and I whipped around to meet the twitchy eyes of General Kuw. "You're coming with us!" he roared.

I looked at my arm, his strong hands digging into my flesh, and then everything around me became a hot blue. I balled the fist of my left hand and smashed it into his face. My fist connected with his teeth and nose and I felt what must have been several of my fingers snap with the strength of it. I brought my fist back and punched him again and he stumbled to the side, letting me go. "Argh!" he grunted, pressing his hand to his face. But even then, he'd brought up his weapon from inside his uniform. *So they'd come to this meeting armed,* I thought, staring at him. Then he brought up his other hand and spread his fingers just in time for a blue ball to explode over the shield he'd activated. I turned to see Okwu flying toward General Kuw and the two went tumbling in the sand.

Pain radiated from my hand now and I stood there for a moment, stunned more by my actions than the state of my mangled fingers. I'd never hit anyone in my entire life. Shuddering with adrenaline, I held my hand up. My middle and index fingers had broken completely enough to show jagged bones. I looked around, dazed. General Kuw was fleeing toward the Khoush ships. Okwu was fighting off barrages of fire bullets with its shield.

It was a strange moment as both the Khoush and Meduse fled toward their armies, leaving me standing there alone. Mwinyi had rushed off while I had been talking to do something I had no time to consider now. Okwu was being pushed back toward the Meduse ships as the Khoush shot at him. I heard Mwinyi yell from nearby and saw Okwu dodge several fire bullets to rush toward me. It came from both sides at once, as the Khoush and the Meduse threw aside what their leaders had just agreed on—the truce.

Who had shot at the Meduse chief to start it all? I will never know. What I did know was that I'd seen the face of the Khoush king when the Meduse chief was shot and it was a face of astonishment and despair. He didn't know; he hadn't wanted this. The rest was reaction. And in their reaction, they all forgot about me. They forgot I was standing there, between their sides as they shot at each other.

Red fire balls and blue searing waves of light flew past me, filling the air. The smell of smoke, incineration, the very air around me began to burn. Rakumi, who was standing where my brother's garden had been, fell as her head was blown clean off. The sound of fireballs zipping past my ears. I coughed and stumbled. Then I felt something punch me in the chest, then my left leg, and then I don't know. I don't know. I screamed. I was flying. The pain bloomed all around me, within me. Now I was moaning, rolling in the dry dirt.

Okwu was on me and everything became blue and muffled. *Binti,* I heard it say to me. *Hold on.* Okwu pressed us both to the ground as the world around us exploded. I felt Okwu shudder as something smashed near it and burst into flames. Then it was as if the fight itself began to rise. I saw it happening and at first thought I was falling. But no, it was the ships of the Khoush and Meduse. They were taking the fight to the skies and probably into space.

Just as quickly as it began, it was over. At least, on Himba soil. Not over, elsewhere. I could hear the battle raging high above and something huge crashed to the ground nearby.

I could not tell, for Okwu was still holding me inside its body. As Okwu lifted off me, I felt myself fading. I could actually *hear* my blood draining into the desert sand beneath me. My back stung in a distant way. My chest was wet and cool, open. My legs, whether they were just torn up or actually torn off, were gone.

Limply, I raised my arm and let it drop to my nose. I sniffed the *otjize* on it and it smelled like home. I heard Mwinyi calling me as he fell to his knees beside me. He was shaking and shaking, his eyes wild. His beautiful bushy hair covered with dust and sand. But I was smelling home. I closed my eyes.

Death is always news.

Chapter 6

Girl

Mwinyi was screaming.

He looked down at her again and kept screaming and screaming and screaming. Her chest was smashed and burned open, bone, sinew, and flesh, red, yellow, and white. Her legs were each a mangle of meat. Her left arm had been blown off. Only her right arm, face, and tentacles were untouched.

Mwinyi had been at what was left of the Root when it all fell apart. He'd turned and seen the Meduse chief and Khoush king both looking at Binti with awe and respect. He'd heard Binti laughing. He'd been proud. He'd seen the leaders walking away. Then he'd turned to what he'd come to see and it had all happened behind his back. By the time he reached her, she was gone.

Okwu floated on Binti's other side, its tentacles touching her torn-up arm and pulling back, touching and pulling back. It could feel the battle happening above, but it stayed with Binti, allowing the others to know that the one who'd become family through war had been killed. They fought harder and angrier because Okwu stayed, because Okwu felt.

Mwinyi looked up, his mouth in an open wail. He was so numb that the sight of the raffia monster running wildly toward him did not startle him. It roared, shoved Mwinyi aside with long sticklike hands, and threw off its head of wooden faces. Mwinyi fell to the side and then stared back at the creature. Not creature, Night Masquerade. The Night Masquerade was mourning Binti.

~

Dele had forgotten all protocol. Last year he'd been initiated into the secret society through which the Night Masquerade spoke. He'd joined just after Binti had left. Learning the chants from the elder men, taking in the smoke from the burned branch of an Undying tree, and seeing the friends of the Seven had all helped him forget about Binti. Then he'd been tapped for grooming as the next Himba chief. He'd been so proud and felt strong, though he hated the scratchy beard he'd had to grow. Throughout, however, no matter how hard he'd worked to forget her, he'd sorely missed Binti.

Days ago, during a meditation with the elders, the elders had all agreed that Binti should see the Night Masquerade. Chief Kapika had been the one in costume standing outside her window. Dele had hated this; Binti was a girl and she'd abandoned her own destiny. And the elders hadn't even bothered telling him Chief Kapika had decided to show Binti the Night Masquerade again yesterday.

However, last night during the *Okuruwo* meeting, Dele had had a change of heart about Binti. He'd listened to her speak, watched her closely, and realized she *was* the Binti he'd known all his life and she was amazing. The elders were the elders for a reason. Even in their own bias, they'd still been able to see and admit to each other what he couldn't up to now . . . but the elders were deeply flawed, too. Hours ago, he'd joined them in a second meeting, this time in the quiet of the desert a mile from Osemba. Dele had thought they were just gathering to go to the Root as a group. When the elders had all agreed to forgo brokering a truce and to sacrifice Binti instead, Dele couldn't believe it.

And so, he'd stolen the Night Masquerade costume. The moment he put it on, he knew what he was to do. And because when a man wears a spiritual costume, he is not himself, Dele found it easy to go to the Root. And there he placed himself where she would see him, hoping she would be encouraged.

And Binti *had* succeeded. He'd seen it even from where he stood on the road. She'd channeled deep culture! He'd felt the power of it shivering through the ground, into his feet, halfway up his legs like electricity, like current. Like almost all the other kids in Osemba, he didn't know how to call up current. He'd only watched Binti do it over the years, glad the practice wasn't his calling. Now, he was watching her do what only a handful had ever done in Himba history. And she used it to convince the leaders of the Khoush and Meduse people to stop fighting for good. She had truly been Osemba's master harmonizer.

Dele stared down at her face now. So beautiful, though the *otjize* on her face was partially rubbed off, her strange tentacles spread over the sand. Limp. It came from deep within his soul, the keening. He threw his head back and opened his mouth wide, tears dribbling from the sides of his eyes. The horror of it squeezed at his heart. He threw aside the leather gloves that made his hands long and stick-like and tore at the Night Masquerade costume, pulling at the raffia, tearing at the blue-and-red cloth.

~

Mwinyi stood up and walked away, his blue garments darkened with Binti's blood and his eyes toward the sky. The fighting had moved toward Khoushland and that was best for them.

"Okwu," he called, hoarsely.

"Yes," the Meduse said, floating over to him.

Behind them, the only Himba Council member to show up continued to scream and scream, his voice rolling across the now empty desert.

"I think we should take her into space," Mwinyi told Okwu. "That's where she belongs. Not here."

"How?" Okwu asked. "The launch port is that way, where the fighting is happening. I don't think . . ."

"Not from the launch port," Mwinyi said, shaking his head.

"A Meduse ship?" Okwu suggested. "They will understand. We set our dead free in space too."

"No," he said firmly. "I have a better plan." He paused, shutting his eyes as despair tried to take him again. "I . . . I know exactly where to take her, too. Will you come?"

"Yes," it said.

"They would never have listened to us," Dele sobbed from behind them. He was holding Binti's only remaining hand.

"Is that why you left her to die?" Mwinyi snapped.

"I didn't," Dele said. "I tried. I didn't agree with the rest of them. But I am just an apprentice; I wasn't even supposed to be speaking. But I did. 'We don't abandon our own,' I said. They said she was no longer one of us and then I was told to be quiet. And none . . . none of them believed they could really evoke deep culture. They didn't believe in . . . they had no hope. The chief said the Khoush would never listen to the Himba because they don't respect us." He squeezed his eyes shut at this as if in physical pain.

"But they respected Binti," Mwinyi said. "The Khoush and Meduse. Then they forgot about her."

Dele looked at Binti and started to sob again.

"Come," Mwinyi snapped. "If you want to do something that would have pleased her, come. Okwu, come."

Mwinyi walked to the wooden foundation of the Root

without looking to see if they were following. With each step he took, he saw more. It was breathtaking, never had he experienced anything like this before. He could *see* where they were, through his feet. All it had taken was for the one he had come to love so much in a matter of days to get torn apart by two irrational peoples.

He stopped at the place where he'd kicked off his sandals. They lay there like the ripped-off wings of a sand beetle. Okwu hovered on one side of him and Dele stood on the other as they looked down at the charred remains of the Root. Mwinyi breathed a sigh of relief. With his feet he could see much. The zinariya had shown him relatives who had this ability in the past. It was called "deep grounding" and it always kicked in when one "walked far enough."

He held his hands up for a moment, preparing to send word through the zinariya, but then he noticed that already coming in all around him were messages from the Ariya, Binti's grandmother, his parents, his brothers, several of his friends, people. The Enyi Zinariya knew what had happened somehow. He had not sent word himself. How did they know already?

"Just stand beside me," Mwinyi said to Okwu and Dele. How could he explain? So he did not. The storm had awakened it and though the storm had passed, he could still feel it vibrating through his exposed feet. The Root's foundation had been made on the dead root of an Undying tree. At least, they'd thought it had been dead. The inside of one of the roots had been hollowed out and made into the house's cellar.

Like Binti, Mwinyi was also a master harmonizer. And his ability was communication in a different way; he could speak to those who were alive. So just as he'd been able to speak with Okwu in a way that allowed him to locate where it had been hurt and where it was best to slather the *otjize,* he'd been able to speak to the living Undying tree that was the Root's foundation.

Dele looked back at Binti's body, lying there alone, and then at her friend, the desert savage named Mwinyi. His bushy hair was a strange red brown, freed like a dust storm and full of dust like . . . a dust storm. His skin was dark like Binti's, but where he'd never seen Binti's skin tone as a marker of being uncivilized, everything about Mwinyi said savage. And so when Mwinyi bent down and placed his hands on the dense charred wood and the ground began to shudder, Dele shouted, "Stop it! What are you doing?" because whatever it was *had* to be wrong.

Okwu watched Mwinyi closely. The human reminded it so much of Binti. *Harmonizers are the same,* Okwu thought. And from a distance, it felt many others of its kind agree with it. It stayed there and waited.

Chapter 7

The Root

A tree with strong roots laughs at storms.

Mwinyi could not remember who said this but he'd heard it often as a child. Never did he imagine the proverb was so literally true. The ground was shuddering as he held his hand to the foundation and repeated over and over, "Let go, please. Let go, let go. Please."

The moment he heard the sound of cracking, he said, "Dele, go!"

"What? Where?" Dele asked. "What is . . . what is happening? What are you doing?"

"Go where the cellar is," Mwinyi said. "You know this house better than I."

"I see it," Okwu said, floating onto the charred foundation.

Mwinyi and Dele followed it. Mwinyi gasped, ran to the spot, and stared. He shut his eyes, as Dele knelt down beside him. Mwinyi could hear the plant's voice in his head now and it was so broad that his head pounded and his vision blurred. It spoke no words he could understand, but there was relief and a sigh. Mwinyi waited as he heard more cracking and then the sound of Dele grunting and pulling and kicking.

Mwinyi held his breath, his eyes closed as he waited a little longer. He saw them with his feet. Then he heard other voices and he sank to the ground, his head in his hands. Binti should have lived to see this. How ecstatic she would have been to know that every single one of her family members was alive and well.

~

Dele had lain on his belly, reached down, and one by one pulled them out. Mother, father, sisters, brothers, nieces, nephews, cousins, and even a few family friends. They ran about, jumped and sang and danced with joy. They didn't care that their skin and hair were nearly free of *otjize*. They kneeled and prayed to the Seven. Sobbing and hugging. Binti's father was the only one who could speak through his joy. He explained to Mwinyi about how they'd all fled into the large cellar and when the Root had been attacked and set aflame, something had made it react as one of the family. It enclosed and protected. And inside the Root, there had not only been supplies that they could eat, but pods of water that grew from the walls of the cellar.

"The Root is true Himba," Binti's father said.

Then he asked, "Where is Binti?"

~

The sun shone bright now and the war happening over Khoushland and in space just outside of the Earth's atmosphere felt more and more distant. It was not the Himba's war, and so for the time being, they were not concerned. News spread fast about Binti and her family's survival through word of mouth. And now that they were out of the protective cellar, they could reach people with their astrolabes, too. Soon a large crowd had gathered at the Root, yes, now it was the Root, again. They brought joyous jars of *otjize* and baskets of food. Home or no home, the Root had been burned, but its foundation was alive and well and strong, as were those who'd lived in it.

Most feared Okwu, but Binti's father stayed at its side well into the day, forcing people to look at and speak to it when they came to wish Binti's father their condolences. Binti's mother stayed with Binti at the place where Binti had fallen. She'd placed a red blanket of mourning over Binti's body, as she hummed to herself and rocked back and forth to keep from tearing her hair out.

Over and over, Mwinyi told Binti's family and those who came about what Binti had tried to do and what she died for. Mwinyi watched their faces; all of them looked upon him as if he were a wild man who had something they wanted—especially Binti's older siblings. Still, Mwinyi told of Binti's bravery and the betrayal of the council and answered their questions because they needed to know.

When the Himba Council arrived at the Root, Mwinyi walked away, heading to Binti's mother. Okwu joined him.

"I don't want to hear any of what they have to say," Mwinyi said.

"We should leave," Okwu said.

"Soon. First, let's talk to her." Mwinyi pointed at Binti's mother. She was cradling Binti's head in her lap and humming. The tips of her long *otjize*-rolled locks dragged on the ground, collecting sand. Even covered with old *otjize,* the bright sun couldn't have been good for her skin. Sweat rolled down her face, dropping into an *otjize*-red damp spot in the sand beneath her.

"Mma Binti," Mwinyi said, sitting before her. When he glanced at Binti's face, every muscle in his body tensed up. When he spoke, his voice quivered. "I'm sorry."

"She didn't know," her mother said. "She didn't know her family was alive. She must have felt . . . homeless."

Mwinyi glanced at Okwu, who floated over. "She loved you all," it said. "She fought for you."

Binti's mother looked at Okwu, then nodded. "My husband . . . he was too afraid to see me do it. He thought I was delirious with panic." She frowned and then continued. "When everything was burning above, *I* was the one who woke the Root," she said. She held up her hand and gracefully made a waving motion. "Everything I see fits together, even all this. I see both sides of the equation, the path that leads to the death of my brightest daughter." She closed her eyes and when a minute passed and she still had not opened them, Mwinyi was about to get up. Her eyes suddenly flew open and she was looking intensely at Mwinyi.

"Are . . . are you alright, Mma Binti?"

"No," she whispered. After a pause, she said, "You have eyes like hers."

"I'm a harmonizer," he said.

She nodded, vaguely, looking down at Binti. "You know, those equations that Binti and her father work to create current, I can *see* just by opening my eyes. Binti got some of this, but she has trained it toward current. I have no training, I just see it. At the door, the center of the cellar, then the wall, that was where the spot was. While everyone cowered in the center, moving from the walls where the heat and smoke were coming through, I went to the place directly across from the door. Across the diameter. I could see the line. Do you know plants can do math? They measure what they need to survive and thrive. The Root has survived long.

"The Root had a spot. I could wake it, if I gave from my own life force. We all have current running through us, that's why we are alive." She held up her right hand. The palm was an angry red and covered with crusty blisters. Mwinyi gasped, reaching for her, but she pulled her hand away. "That's how the Root knew to protect its people." She pressed her hand to her chest. "But once it closed, it would not open. You saved us too, Mwinyi."

She took his hand with her uninjured one. Then she quickly let go and her eyes fell back to Binti.

"We want to take her," Mwinyi said, after she'd been

quiet for several moments. "Into space. That's where she always said she felt most . . . natural." When Binti's mother didn't say anything, Mwinyi continued, "She once told me that she thought she needed to go to the rings of Saturn; that a vision was calling her there. That's where I think we should take her."

He waited, holding his breath.

"Why'd you come here?" she finally asked, without looking up. "Why couldn't you both have just stayed there?"

Mwinyi sighed and sat down across from her. He looked at her puffy red downcast eyes and then slowly reached forward and took the hand that was not holding Binti's remaining hand. "I didn't want to come," he admitted. "It wasn't safe. And even as I rode out with her, I felt something was off . . . with her." He looked cautiously at her mother. She still looked down at her daughter. He continued. "She's a master harmonizer, but what harmony did she bring? I couldn't understand her. She seemed broken." He held his breath. But now that he had started, he might as well finish. "But Binti was . . . was more than a harmonizer, I realized. There is no word for her yet. I knew she'd do something amazing."

"But she didn't," her mother said, looking up at him. "She failed." Her face was naked as tears ran from her eyes.

"She didn't fail, Khoush and Meduse did," Okwu said, from behind Mwinyi.

"Binti did what she was born to do. Even the most ancient of my clan could not have done what she did, been what she was, carried it as she did, and understand, my people are old and advanced." He waited and when she didn't speak her mind, he continued, "You Himba know us as the Desert People. We are—"

"The Enyi Zinariya," she said. "I know. I married one of you . . . who also was a master harmonizer." She looked down at Binti. "I always knew that she was meant to do something great. We knew when she got into Oomza Uni, though she didn't know we knew. I knew when she agreed to the interview. Her father was so angry when she left . . . but I . . . I wasn't. I understood." She leaned down and kissed Binti on the forehead and then her shoulders slumped. She looked up at Mwinyi, waiting.

"Can we take her?" he asked again.

"How?"

"By neither Meduse ship nor Khoush," Mwinyi said. "Don't worry about that."

"To the rings of Saturn?"

He nodded. "It's where she wanted to go next."

She stared at Mwinyi for a long time and he did not look away. This was part of their conversation and Mwinyi relaxed into it, letting Binti's mother in. When she finally looked away, her tears had stopped and she smiled weakly to herself. "The women will have to prepare her, first," she said. "But, yes. Take my daughter where she wanted to go."

~

Binti's brothers erected a tent around her, so that no one would see. Then the women spent the rest of the day preparing Binti, right there on the spot where she'd fallen. The chief of surgery, a stern woman who'd tied back her waist-length *otjize*-heavy locks, repaired Binti's insides as best she could and sewed up her chest, and the opened wound left where her arm had been. They bathed her with water from the Sacred Well. They massaged her flesh with sweet-smelling oil and then applied Binti's mother's *otjize*. And lastly, one of the seamstresses presented the "homecoming" dress she's sewn for Binti as the other women worked. The long dress was the red-orange color of the richest *otjize,* with a light blue sash that the seamstress refused to explain.

When Binti was ready, she was placed on top of the costume of the Night Masquerade. Because so many had seen it, those in the secret society would need to create a new, different one. And both Chief Kapika and Dele felt that it belonged to Binti now, anyway. Binti was change, she was revolution, she was heroism. She was more Night Masquerade than anyone had ever been. Then the chief called a ceremony and had a girl climb a palm tree and cut a large leaf. The traditional leaf was sent from home to home, though messages about it via astrolabe traveled faster.

The evening was windy again. Another electrical storm thrashed itself out somewhere deep in the desert, but close enough to give the air a tangy charged smell. Dele spoke the words of dedication and love to what was probably all of Osemba. And as he spoke of his best friend, his voice loud and strong, from the west, in Khoushland, the distant boom and crack of Khoush and Meduse arsenal finding purchase distracted many. The darkening sky flickered as the Khoush and Meduse battled in space above.

All the while, Mwinyi and Okwu stayed on the outskirts of it all. These rituals were not for them. Not really. These were not their people and, in Mwinyi's opinion, much of this was done out of guilt. As they'd waited, Mwinyi had spoken with everyone back home and then he'd stopped because they were so angry and disgusted with the Himba and he didn't really want to hear them express what he was working not to feel. He'd only told Binti's grandmother of the plan.

"Take her home," was all she said.

Come evening, everyone had said their goodbyes and all that remained were Binti's parents, siblings, Mwinyi, and Okwu. Boxes of packaged foods, including dates, green plantains, flour, stacks of a dried edible weed, boxes of roasted grasshoppers Okwu liked to eat, and other supplies were stacked beside Okwu. They were quiet as they stood around Binti's body in the dark. Mwinyi walked away from them all and stood on what was left of the Root. It still smelled of smoke here and some of the pieces crumbled beneath his feet as he walked and listened.

Through his rough feet he saw many things of the past, when the Root had stood. He saw Binti's mother singing mathematical equations to a large grasshopper that had flown into the cellar, holding her hand out for it to land, and watching it slowly fold its beautifully decorative wings as if to show her its mathematical pattern. He saw Binti arguing with her sister so many years ago about a dance and her sister laughing and rolling her eyes. He saw Binti's father sneak into the cellar to use the zinariya to speak to his mother.

Mwinyi opened his eyes and took a deep breath. He loved being able to "ground," absolutely loved it. The universe was a singing connection of stories and he could listen to that song anywhere he went now. "I'll never wear shoes again," he whispered to himself.

He looked to the stars and then smiled. It was time. And sure enough, there were the lights. She was coming. He looked to the group; several of Binti's sisters had begun to cry. Binti's father was standing with his head in his hands. And her mother was looking mournfully at Mwinyi.

Shrimplike in its shape, the Miri 12 luminesced a deep purple blue in the night, with pink highlights running around the windows of its front. But this wasn't Third Fish. This Miri 12 was nowhere near as large, barely the size of the Root when the Root had been intact. This was Third Fish's baby, New Fish. She zipped swiftly around them in a large circle, playfully blowing them all with warm air, though remaining careful not to blow dust on Binti's body.

"Praise the Seven," Mwinyi whispered.

He'd called Third Fish last night when he'd walked out into the desert from the Osemba House. The great elephant

Arewhana, who'd taught him so much (including how to call large animals from afar), would have been proud. Unlike Binti, Mwinyi hadn't been so confident that things would turn out well with the truce. And so he'd used his harmonizing skill to reach out to Third Fish. The first time had been yesterday, as he stood near the lake. Surprisingly she responded in her deep soft voice. She said she'd help if he needed help, that she was nearby. All he'd have to do was call.

And he'd called. And Third Fish had sent her child to take this sad journey.

~

The goodbyes were quick.

Binti's brothers had carefully picked up her body and taken her into New Fish. Soft blue lights on the soft ship floor guided them to where New Fish wanted her kept. Mwinyi assured them that this was fine, and no one questioned the ship's decision. In actuality, Mwinyi knew as little as any of them, aside from what the ship told him in its strange voice. But he was struggling with the very idea of leaving Earth, so the smoother and faster this departure went, the better. Mwinyi took one step onto New Fish, stopped, rubbed his now throbbing temples, and put his sandals right back on. Best to deal with his first experience of leaving Earth before anything else.

The room New Fish led them to was one of its upper breathing rooms, a place full of green leafy Earth plants that were just taking root in the newly born creature. The floor here was a soft, almost raw-looking pink and this was where New Fish told Mwinyi they should set Binti. Mwinyi immediately thought of Binti's grandmother's room where she kept so many plants she'd discovered and nurtured. The smell here was wet sand during rare rains, water-filled leaves, the ozone smell after thunderstorms, and the soil Binti's grandmother collected from the bottom of wells and used to pot plants. It was fresh and full of life here.

Okwu had squeezed itself into the room, but moved out of it a moment later. "She loved this place in the Third Fish," it told Mwinyi and Binti's brothers as they put her down. "She said she liked the damp, the warmth, and the smell. All I smell are microbes." Then it left to explore the rest of the ship.

Binti's brothers Omeva and Bena didn't linger either. They clearly wanted to leave the room, to get away from their little sister's body. Binti's mother had to be taken away by Binti's father before the ship took off, for she'd begun to tear at her clothes and had even torn one of her locks out. The sisters had started to keen and sing a mournful song that Mwinyi never wanted to hear again and the other Himba people only stood there staring, still in shock about all that had happened in the last twenty-four hours.

Mwinyi remained in the room for a while longer, then he left, and the door slid shut behind him.

Chapter 8

Space Is the Place

"I'm glad to leave Earth," Okwu said. It exhaled a large cloud of gas as it looked out the window.

Mwinyi still clung to the pillar in the middle of the pilot chamber. He had been born and raised in the desert and never had he dreamed of leaving the Earth. He'd been happy protecting his people when they went on journeys across the desert and communing with the various peoples of the desert, from fox to dog to hawk to ant. His life had been simple; however, the moment Binti entered his life, he'd known that simplicity was over.

He would never be able to describe what it felt like to sit strapped to one of New Fish's strangely molded chairs and leave the Earth. Even an hour later, he wasn't able to speak. Okwu seemed to understand this, for it left Mwinyi alone as it hovered near one of the wall-size windows in New Fish's cockpit. Okwu hadn't needed to strap itself down and didn't seem to be affected by the change in air pressure or gravity as the ship balanced out its insides to reflect an Earth-like atmosphere.

When Mwinyi did speak, it was to New Fish.

After? it asked, hours later as Mwinyi slept in the large room near New Fish's top called the Star Chamber. It felt like a vibration on his back that formed words he could understand in his mind.

Mwinyi had chosen this room because its ceiling was all window and he could rest on his back and look into space in a way similar to how he looked into the sky when he went off into the desert alone back home. He'd been asleep on the floor, which was so soft that he didn't need his mat. He rolled over, resting his hands on the purple luminescent floor. "After what?" he said aloud.

After Saturn. After we set her free.

"Oh," he said, his shoulder slumping as it all came back to him. The deep exhausted sleep he'd been in gave him respite from Binti's death and the fact that he'd just left his home without mentally preparing to do any such thing. "I . . . Okwu says we should go to his school. Oomza Uni."

That is far.

"I know."

What do you *want?*

He sighed. "It's fine. What do *you* want?"

The ship vibrated, the ceiling creaking and the floor flickering with stripes of blue purple and pink. Glee. Mwinyi smiled. *I want to fly,* New Fish said. *Go far.*

Mwinyi lay on his belly, his hands still pressed to New Fish. "Can I go back to sleep now?"

Yes. But . . . no. Will you please tell me about Binti? My mother told me much. You tell me things too.

And so it was an hour before Mwinyi went back to the escape of sleep, as he told New Fish all he knew about Binti. He even told New Fish how much he loved her and finished by surprising himself. He *did* want to go to Oomza Uni. It was far from the home he wanted to return to, but it was where a part of Binti also lived. He told New Fish that he wanted to meet her friends and her mathematics professor. He wanted to see where she collected the clay she used for *otjize*. And when he finally did lie on New Fish's soft welcoming flesh, he slept even more deeply than before and the dreams he had were full of beautiful flashing colors and a soothing hum.

~

Neither Mwinyi nor Okwu could bring themselves to go into that room. As the days passed and they got closer to Saturn, the idea became less and less savory. For Mwinyi, he could only imagine what her body looked like or how she smelled in that warm jungly room full of plants, soil, and according to Okwu, microbes.

For Okwu, opening that room meant it was time to set Binti free. Neither Okwu nor its fellow Meduse, who were most of the time thirsty with war, wanted to send this peaceful girl human on a journey on which they could not join her. And Okwu couldn't bear to part with its partner. Not at this time, when things had gone so far.

Nevertheless, when the equivalent of three days had passed and New Fish excitedly told Mwinyi that they were approaching Saturn's ring in an hour, it was time to face reality.

It's time, New Fish excitedly rumbled.

Mwinyi, who'd been watching Saturn approach through the star room window, felt his spirits drop. New Fish had been moving and now she came to a stop, hovering in deep space. Waiting. Mwinyi found himself a bit annoyed with the ship's overly cheerful demeanor, especially in the last twenty-four hours. But he said nothing. New Fish was a young living ship, a creature born to travel far and fast, and she was in space for the first time. How could he blame her for feeling free and adventurous?

The walkway to the breathing chamber was narrow and the left side was lined with windows that showed the blackness outside. Okwu led the way.

"I don't know if I'm ready for this," Mwinyi said.

"No one is ever ready for such a thing," Okwu said. "But we will send her on her way to her next journey."

Mwinyi saw Binti's faces in his mind, with and without *otjize*. He felt his heart would break a second time.

"Keep moving," Okwu said.

When they reached the breathing chamber, Okwu

went right in. Mwinyi hesitated and then followed. He shut the door behind him. There, among the lovely plants, irrigated by clean waters that ran throughout New Fish to other breathing rooms, was Binti's body wrapped in its red soft cloth, lying on the costume of the Night Masquerade.

"She looks the same," Okwu said and Mwinyi shivered, understanding exactly what it meant. Her body wasn't bloating yet. Making an effort not to look at the unnerving Night Masquerade costume, Mwinyi put the transporter on the floor beside her body and powered it up. Within a second, it shivered and then buzzed softly. Binti's wrapped body and the Night Masquerade costume lifted off the ground.

Mwinyi sighed. "Okay," he muttered, his voice thick. He gave her a gentle push and she smoothly glided toward the door. Mwinyi stopped her, looking at Okwu.

"What?" it said. "We must do this fast." It moved quickly toward the door. The door slid open and Okwu squeezed through. Just outside the room, Mwinyi could see it let out a great blast of gas and inhale it back in. Then it let some out again, as it moved away from the door.

Mwinyi looked down at Binti. He inhaled and held his breath; he didn't want to smell her. He reached down. He had to see her face one more time. He did not care if it was bloated from death or even eaten by organisms that lived in the breathing room. He had to see her, to truly say goodbye. He flipped the red cloth aside. He stared. He let out his breath.

Her *okuoko* were writhing like snakes.

~

I was staring back.

Chapter 9

Awake

I was there.

Then I opened my eyes.

"It's all mathematics," I said.

I don't know where the words came from or why I said them. Mwinyi was staring at me, his mouth agape. "Life, the universe, everything." I turned my head to the side and caught a glimpse of the Night Masquerade I lay on. The costume.

Mwinyi reached a hand forward and pulled more of the cloth off me. I looked down too, as he gasped, jumping up and stumbling back. "*Okwu!*" he finally called. "Okwu! Get in here!"

I looked toward the door where Okwu hovered, just outside the room. The moment I laid eyes on it, I saw it float quickly back, leaving a great cloud of its lavender gas as it went. Then I could hear it puffing it out, sucking it back in, puffing it out, sucking it in.

"Binti," Mwinyi whispered. "What . . . is this really you?" He had tears in his eyes, his lips were quivering. I'd been watching him move about the ship for hours. It had been as if I were swimming, rolling, floating in the tree. Then I was pulled into this place, this ship, and it had embraced me with delight. And I'd seen Okwu and Mwinyi moving about, both of them so sad, numb, and quiet. I'd followed them here and opened my eyes.

I sat up as he stared at me. I touched my left arm. I had a left arm. Mwinyi sank to the floor, his back against the slender trunk of a young tree with tough rubbery-looking leaves growing from a hole in the floor. A tree that looked oddly like an Undying tree. *Home,* I thought as I pressed my chest. I remembered most clearly when the Khoush fire bullet hit me in the chest. The punching, then stabbing pain, and once inside me, it had hungrily bitten at me with its fire. I pressed my soft breasts now, beneath the red dress I wore. I rolled to the side and touched the sticklike hand of the Night Masquerade costume. I held it with my left hand, kneading the actual sticks used for the knuckles with my fingers.

I nearly laughed now when I thought back to that moment when I'd stood at my bedroom window staring down at the Night Masquerade that first time. Deep down a tiny, tiny voice in me had wondered if something were wrong with me, if my spirit was that of a man's, not a woman's, because the Night Masquerade never showed itself to girls or women. Even back then I had changed things, and I didn't even know it. When I should have reveled in this gift, instead, I'd seen myself as broken. But couldn't you be broken and still bring change?

I powered down the transporter beside me and it lowered me to the ground. I closed my eyes and said a silent prayer to thank the Seven for Their Mysterious Mystery. Then slowly, my muscles creaking and aching, old *otjize* flaking to the floor, I stood up. I had legs, too. I felt the ship rumble, the leaves, flowers, stems, and branches around us shaking. I felt the ship's voice more than heard it, in every part of me, but especially my chest, left arm, and legs. "*Hello, Binti,*" it said. It spoke in Khoush. Mwinyi looked around and then back at me.

"New Fish is speaking to you, isn't she?" he asked. "I can hear her, but barely."

I nodded.

"Hello," I said aloud, not sure how else to speak to it. "You are New Fish? Is that—"

"*Yes. Third Fish's daughter,*" she said.

"I died," I blurted. "I remember. They had agreed to stop fighting and then something happened and they started fighting anyway. They forgot about me and I got caught in the crossfire. I don't know if Khoush or Meduse killed me . . ." I paused, as more of those moments returned to me. I'd seen flashes of blue and red, felt heat and cold. I'd been shot by Meduse and Khoush alike. "How is it possible that I'm standing in your breathing room looking at Mwinyi. Breathing." I held out my arms to him and immediately he rushed over.

He gathered me in his arms.

"Microbes," I heard Okwu say from the door. It stood in it, filling it up completely as it floated.

"Okwu," I said, feeling my *okuoko* writhe. And for the first time I knew how to do it. I sent the small spark toward it and it popped in a series of blue sparks at its tentacles. Okwu's dome expanded, filling the doorway even more tightly, and then deflated.

"My mother said it would happen if they put you in my breathing chamber, because I am so young," New Fish said. *"That is why she sent me instead of coming herself. She would have broken through the curfew gate they set up for all launch port ships once the fighting started. My mother isn't afraid of her bond to the Khoush. But she knew. And she saw your soul when everything happened on your journey to Oomza Uni. She calls you the 'gentle warrior' and believes our union would bring Miri 12s forward."*

"Union?" I asked. Again, *another* connection.

"What's she saying?" Mwinyi asked. "I can't quite—"

"Shhh," I said to Mwinyi, still holding him.

"Come up to my Star Chamber and I will explain," New Fish said.

~

I sat on the Star Chamber floor looking out the large window before me. This was where Mwinyi had been staying and I could see why. I stared out at the distant Saturn as I drank a second cup of water and finished a bowl of dried meat. The water tasted soily, having been drawn from one of New Fish's wells, and the meat was spicy and tough. It was delicious. I didn't have to ask to know that this was meat someone from my town had supplied for the journey. Goat meat, sliced thin and cured in an Osemba smokehouse.

I had followed Mwinyi up the corridor, marveling at New Fish's young interior design. I soon slowed down, overcome with a thirst and hunger so strong that I felt as if my body were trying to consume itself. By the time we reached the Star Chamber, I'd sat down right there in the middle of the room and could say nothing but "Water," and then when I had that, "Food."

As I ate and drank, things around me cleared and soon I was just chewing on the meat because it was tasty. Mwinyi sat beside me, eating a handful of dates. Okwu hovered near the other wall of windows, chicken bones scattered on the floor beneath it. I'd never actually watched Okwu eat; Okwu liked to go off and eat alone and for a while, I'd wondered if it ate at all. Thus, seeing it consume the roasted chicken it had brought up from storage had been a sight. Meduse eat like delicate old ladies, slowly picking at and drawing in the meat bit by bit with their *okuoko*. Watching it eat had brought me my first real smile since I'd sat up and had a living body to smile with.

"Okay," I finally said, taking one more gulp of water.

"I'm listening." I looked at my right arm, flaking the remaining old *otjize* off to reveal my dark brown skin.

"Wait," Mwinyi said. "Before New Fish speaks to you, Okwu and I want to tell you what happened after you . . . after they killed you." He frowned, a pained look on his face. "I can't believe I can say that to you. 'Killed.'" He let out a breath.

"I know," I said. But somehow, out there in space on New Fish, with a Meduse and an Enyi Zinariya master harmonizer, it all seemed so bizarre, what was the added detail of me coming back from the dead? "When one dies, the Seven take you, no matter who you are. You join the whole again. The wilderness. You don't come back."

"Meduse always come back," Okwu said, quietly. "We reincarnate."

"Do you remember the Seven?" Mwinyi asked, ignoring Okwu. "The Principle Artists of All Things?"

"I do," I said. Seeing the shock on Mwinyi's face and the puff of gas that Okwu blew out amused me. They hadn't expected me to say that; however, I *did* remember. "But tell me what you need to tell me."

When he got to the part about my family, I screamed. I jumped up, knocking over my cup of water. I didn't know where to go, so I just stood there. I just stood there. My chest tight, the heart inside it beating strong again. My legs strong. My flesh naked. My *okuoko,* which were now past my waist, vibrating. I pressed my hands against the sides of my face. Then I lifted my dress to my knees and did my village's fire dance, stamping my feet hard to make my anklets jingle. When I looked at my legs, I saw that I didn't have any anklets. I danced anyway, hearing the jingling in my mind.

"I spoke to the Root," Mwinyi laughingly explained as I danced and danced with joy. "And it opened up. And we were able to get everyone out."

"Everyone," I said, stretching my hands toward the window, toward outer space. "No one was hurt?"

"Everyone was well," Mwinyi said.

I whirled around, ran to him, threw my arms around him, and kissed him long and hard. And through my *okuoko,* I threw a blue spark, the size and shape of a large tomato, at Okwu. I jumped back and began to dance again and when I saw Okwu vibrating its dome with laughter, I danced harder. My family was *alive*! My family was *alive*! The Root was alive, even if the house built on it had been burned to ash. We *survive.*

"How?" I asked.

When Mwinyi told me what my mother had said, I stared at him in awe. "She used her mathematical sight?" I whispered. "My mother, she sees the math in the world, she was born with it. That's where the sharpness of my gift comes from. She was never trained, though. She just used it to protect the family during storms, to fortify the house, sometimes to heal you if you were sick. My mother is so powerful." I laughed to myself, tears welling up in my eyes.

"I can't believe it! Thank the Seven, praise the Seven, the Seven are great, they make circles in the sand!" *That* was why I couldn't see her during my fevered zinariya visions. While everyone else had moved from the walls to get away from the smoke and heat, my mother had gone toward the danger to find the spot that woke the Root's defenses.

"I've contacted my home," Mwinyi added. "They are sending people to meet with the Himba. Your man Dele will lead the meeting with them."

I paused at him referring to Dele as my "man," but quickly moved on. "Dele was there?" I remembered. "Oh! Mwinyi, he was the Night Masquerade! I saw him! I saw him!" I wrapped my arms around myself, tears welling in my eyes.

"The Himba Council *did* betray you," Mwinyi said. "But Dele didn't. He was there as the Night Masquerade to give you hope and strength."

I listened in silence as Mwinyi explained. This part I had to let sink in. The Night Masquerade was a secret society of men? And Dele was in it? A part of me still rejected this. That first time I'd seen it from my bedroom window, it had looked like a creature, not a man in a costume. And what of my uncle and my father who had also seen it? Did they know of the tradition too?

Regardless, I felt good. About everything. The war had begun again, my home would never be what it was, but this, I understood more than ever now, was inevitable. Change was inevitable and where the Seven were involved, so was growth. My family was *alive,* the Enyi Zinariya were going to meet them and help Osemba *survive* and evolve. And if any people knew how to survive and evolve, it was the Enyi Zinariya. Osemba would change and grow.

Dele was not a harmonizer, but he had come of age with me and he had to have learned something about himself after what happened with the Himba Council. He'd just started his apprenticeship to be the next Himba chief and, rigid and traditional as he was, he'd already broken out of the mold when he believed the council had made a mistake. His love and protectiveness of his people was strong enough to push tradition to grow. Dele was ready for what was coming and I felt good about what he'd do.

It was then that I remembered something else and my heart began to pound like crazy because it had already been three days. There was no going back home with ease. I reached into the pocket of my right hip where I had kept it. I wasn't wearing the same dress, but maybe . . . my shoulders slumped. The *edan* pieces and its inner golden ball weren't there. It was lost.

"New Fish," I said. "Okay, I am ready to hear your explanation." I reached into my left front pocket as I sat down. I felt the edge of something sharp. I grinned as I shoved my hand further in and grasped the golden ball. "*Thank the Seven,*" I whispered. "And thank my family."

"*I am young and there wasn't much time,*" New Fish said to me.

Mwinyi was sitting on the floor, with his chest pressed

to it, his arms out as he pressed his palms to the floor. "It's how I hear her clearest," he said when I looked at him questioningly.

I nodded at him and looked at Okwu, who just said, "Tell me when she has finished."

"I don't know much," New Fish continued. *"Most Miri 12s never do this. We don't become more. We are ships because we like to travel, that's what mother said. Until she harbored you. Then she started thinking. Even before Mwinyi called out to her. So she told me about 'deep Miri' and how I had to work it. We have breathing chambers.*

"My mother said that before I was born, my chambers were seeded from her inner plants. Those plants not only produce the gases for us to breathe when we leave planets with breathable atmospheres, but they also carry bacteria, good viruses, and other microorganisms, and these microbes go on to populate every part of my body. But they populate the breathing chamber most passionately when a Miri 12 is new born like me.

"When your body was placed in my chamber, my microbes went to work. You are probably more microbes than human now."

I frowned. "What does that mean? I look and feel like myself. I remember who I am. I was dead, right?"

"That is the 'deep Miri' my mother said would happen. I don't understand it, myself. But they blended with your genes and repaired you, regrew your arm and legs, then pulled you back. There is one thing, though." She stopped talking for a moment and I was relieved. I needed to think.

I was dead. This fact echoed through my brain, ricocheting off the walls and slamming back again and again. *I was dead, I was dead, I was dead.* I remembered joining the Seven. Was I even me now? I was physically more Miri 12 than human. I touched the *okuoko* on my head and my temples throbbed. I raised my hands and typed and pushed the message to Mwinyi with more ease than I'd experienced while on Earth. "Am I still Enyi Zinariya?" I asked. My world stayed steady and there were no voices. I didn't look toward the window to see if there was a tunnel in space or a strange planet bouncing beside Saturn.

"You will always be Enyi Zinariya," he responded, his green words appearing before me in crisp letters. I touched them and they faded away like incense smoke.

"*What is Enyi Zinariya?*" New Fish's words floated at me in bright pink and I gasped.

Mwinyi gasped too.

"Did she send it to you, too?" I asked.

He nodded.

"*I've absorbed some of you, too, Binti,*" she said. And again, the room lit up with the orange-pink color.

"The Enyi Zinariya are my tribe, our tribe," Mwinyi said. "We got our name from the Zinariya people who visited and changed us long ago." He cut his eyes at me and added, "You might know us as 'the Desert People.'"

"*Oh,*" New Fish said. "*Yes, my mother liked to talk about Binti's dark skin, dense hair, and old African face. She said that may be what gave Binti her fight, desert bloods. We weren't even sure if you were really Himba."*

"I am Himba," I snapped.

The room became orange-pink again, and this time stayed that way. Mwinyi rolled his eyes and said, "Yes, yes, Binti, you are Himba. No one's taking that from you."

I frowned even more deeply and turned my back to him, for the moment angry and frustrated with too many things to focus on a response.

"Can I ask you something, New Fish?" Mwinyi said.

"Ask," New Fish said.

"If you were only born a few days ago, how come you can communicate so well?"

The ship's room flashed a soft orange-pink so pleasant that I instantly felt less annoyed. It was the same color as the ntu ntu bugs on Oomza Uni. *"I have been talking to my mother for five Earth years and my mother is old, so very smart. A Miri 12 is 'pregnant' when she is near her time to give birth. And birth is not the beginning for us; it's just a change."*

Mwinyi nodded, looking amazed. "So you have been inside your mother for five years and you two talk?"

"I've been all over the galaxy with my mother, who was born on Earth. But mostly to Earth and Oomza, since my mother has been doing that route since I spawned. This is why I can speak Khoush."

"So you were there when . . . did you know when the Meduse killed everyone on board your mother?"

"Moojh-ha ki-bira," she said. "*Yes. My mother said she and I should stay quiet until we reached Oomza. That was the first time in my entire life that I had nightmares when I slept.*"

We were quiet for a few moments. Then I asked, "What was it that you were going to tell me? You said there was something I needed to know."

"*I may have spoken too soon,*" New Fish said, after a moment. "*You've just woken. You've just eaten.*"

"I'm fine," I said impatiently. "Please, tell it all to me now. I'd rather be shocked all at once. Tell me everything." I was breathing heavily. I'd had a strange feeling as New Fish spoke to me. It was leading up to telling me something big. "Should I let myself tree first? When I do that I can handle any shock, any—"

"*No. Don't tree. That won't help.*"

"Why?"

"You will see."

And then I did.

Suddenly, the Star Chamber, Mwinyi, Okwu, everything was gone. I was in space. Infinite blackness was all around me, except for Saturn, pale and blue in the distance, and the sun in the other direction. The blue-pink bioluminescent light of New Fish seemed to radiate from me. With each second, I became more aware of this and then I began to fall. And as I fell faster and faster, I didn't have any arms with which to flail and I began to panic. I started screaming. I shuddered and my scream came out as a deep groan.

Relax, I heard New Fish say. She spoke in my head. *Just be. You are safe.*

What's . . . what's happening to me? I shouted. Again, my voice was just a rumble. I could feel myself shaking, shuddering. Not myself, not my body. New Fish's body.

Your body too, now, she said.

The word she'd said before came back to me, "union."

Your body is partially me, she said. *That's how the deep Miri brought you back. And in turn, I am partially you.*

As I relaxed, I realized that for the first time, I could do something I'd always dreamed of when I was little. I was in space with no suit, in no ship, and I wasn't dying. This was my chance to do that for real. I let myself be New Fish and noticed that I was just floating. There was no up or down. I felt neither cool nor hot, though I felt a warmth from within and that was enough. I looked straight ahead at Saturn.

The Seven are Great, I said.

They are.

How do I—

But then I was doing it. I was flying forward. I flipped and flew what my body perceived as down. I laughed with glee and flew fast and stopped and flew faster and stopped. The feeling of floating in space made me euphoric. It was such freedom. I was doing a barrel roll when I remembered Mwinyi and Okwu were on the ship and in that moment, something odd happened. I could feel myself gradually slow down. Then I was back inside, looking down at Okwu and Mwinyi in the Star Chamber. Mwinyi was hanging on to a pole, a look of horror on his face. Okwu was simply hovering, now on the other side of the room. Then I was back in my body, sitting cross-legged on the floor in the middle of the room. I looked around, blinking.

"Binti? Can you hear me now?" Mwinyi shouted.

"Huh?" I said, resting a hand on the soft floor.

"You nearly killed us!" Mwinyi said.

"She nearly killed *you*. Not me," Okwu said. "And I caught you. You are fine."

Mwinyi frowned angrily at Okwu.

"Sorry," I said. When I stretched my legs, I had to use some effort because the bottoms of my legs were adhered to New Fish's surface with some kind of mucus. This was why I hadn't been thrashed around like Mwinyi. I pulled some of the gummy substance from the backs of my legs and dress. "Can you become me as I became you?" I asked New Fish.

"It is not that you became me. I'm a Miri 12, it is how we connect. But no, I would not connect with you in that way. You don't have the capacity."

I was too tired to address New Fish's quiet condescension.

"The final thing I must tell you is that if we were on Earth, because you've taken so much from me to live, you and I can never be too far from one another."

I yawned. "Why? What would happen?"

"I don't know."

"How far is too far?"

"I'm not sure," she said. *"When my mother sent me, she couldn't answer every question I had. With all the shooting near the launch port, I was more worried about getting shot down on my way to you."*

"It's alright," I said, standing up. I didn't have the energy to wonder about this, either. Not at the moment. Plus we were in space and I wasn't going to move away from New Fish any time soon. And where were we going now, anyway? I needed to rest first.

Chapter 10

Stones of Saturn

"We're going to go through Saturn's ring," I said hours later, after a long nap. "I'm not discussing it. Then we turn around and head to Oomza Uni, as you planned."

"Okay," was all Mwinyi replied.

Okwu said nothing, nor did New Fish. I turned back to the large window feeling satisfied with myself. I'd been ready to argue with all of them and it was nice to get what I wanted so easily.

After waking from my nine hours of sleep, I'd connected with New Fish again. This time, I did it on my own. New Fish might have been asleep, for I didn't sense her presence at all. It was just me out there as a living ship. I felt the air in my breathing chambers, the strength in my body. I even felt Mwinyi standing in the corner, moving his hands about as he talked to several people in the desert on Earth and Okwu in the room below. Okwu was not talking to the other Meduse on Earth, it was observing. When connected to New Fish, I brought all my skills with me. I considered attempting to tree while connected, but decided against it. The results of treeing were affected by size, and who knew what I'd call up.

As I floated out there in space, enjoying the absolute quiet, I gazed at Saturn. We were near enough to see its shape and rings. Saturn was close enough to reach within hours, even if New Fish took her time. This was when I'd decided we should go.

"*My mother says* edans *are unpredictable,*" New Fish said now. "*She said yours especially could have its own consciousness.*"

But I wanted to see. Had to see. After all I'd been through, I needed to get to the bottom of this mystery. "I don't care," I snapped. "We are going even if I have to hijack you and force you to fly there."

"*You can't,*" New Fish said.

"I'll try," I said.

"*Go ahead,*" New Fish goaded.

"Only if I have to," I said.

"Ugh, will you both shut up?" Mwinyi snapped, taking his hands from the floor. "No one's fighting you on this, Binti. No need to be like that."

Okwu vibrated its dome and blew out so much gas that both Mwinyi and I started coughing.

I got up and went to the breathing room where I'd lain for days. I picked up the Night Masquerade costume. Then I went down to another of New Fish's breathing rooms. I'd felt this one when I was connected to New Fish. When I went inside, the light in here was very similar to the midday desert sun and when I saw the trees, I knew why. There were ten of them, some were saplings, several were small nearly matured trees, and one of them was fully matured, reaching the ceiling and bending a bit to the side. Undying trees! The saplings looked recently potted inside the flesh of New Fish, and the mature one had roots that extended down into New Fish like nerves. The floor was slightly transparent and I could see the roots going deep. These trees had all been growing while New Fish was in utero.

Not for the first time, I wondered if Third Fish was also psychic. And did that mean New Fish was too? There were other plants here that I recognized from Osemba as well. Plants that were usually peopled with land crabs, lizards, and other creatures because these plants attracted insects and smaller life forms. They attracted life. The floor here was dry, even coated with a layer of sand in some places. I touched the trees' leaves, which were all rough with what the Himba called "life salt," a pinkish grainy substance that healers used to cure and treat all sorts of ailments.

I tasted it now and it invigorated my tongue. When I'd first found my *edan,* my father brought it to his tongue to taste what kind of metal it was. He hadn't been able to identify it, but he'd said it tasted like life salt. I laid out the Night Masquerade on the floor and looked at it. The smiling side of its many-masked head stared back at me. I shivered with residual disbelief that this was the costume of the Night Masquerade, that it *was* a costume. I sat down facing its head. Then I brought out the *edan* pieces and the golden ball.

I brought the ball to my face and looked at its fingerprint-like surface closely. Then I held up my left hand and looked at my fingerprints. Had the print on my left middle and index fingers always matched the ones on the ball? I'd never compared them before I'd lost my left arm, so who knows. But now they matched perfectly and this didn't surprise me. Nor had the presence of Undying trees.

Holding it on the palm of my right hand, I touched my index and middle fingers to their spots on the golden ball and immediately it began to hum and vibrate. "Okay," I whispered, placing it on the floor before me. If it weren't for the sand, the ball would have begun to roll away. Softly, I whispered, "$(x—h)^2 + (y—k)^2 = r^2$" and the equation floated from my lips in a way that reminded me of the zinariya. It was even my color of red. I chose the equation for circles because it was all coming back around and around and around. And the equation stretched into a circle as I let myself tree, surrounding me before it faded away.

The moment I called up a thick strong current, blue like Okwu, the Undying trees in the room began to vibrate too. It was the same way they reacted to lightning storms back home. As I led the current to the golden ball, the trees' vibrations had become so fast and steady that they began to hum. Slowly, the ball rose. It hovered before my eyes, a foot away, and began to slowly rotate.

As I climbed higher up the tree, I thought about the Zinariya. They'd come to a quiet part of Africa, where the people lived very close to the desert. Close and isolated enough that the people in those small communities knew how to keep a secret. And thus, the rest of the world never knew of the tall, humanoid gold people who loved the way the sun reacted with Earth's atmosphere there. They saw this small patch of Earth as a vacation spot and the people they met didn't mind. Their friendship started with a girl named Kande. In many ways, she was like me. What Kande started had eventually made the people in this small town more.

Made the Zinariya more.

They left an *edan*. No instructions. No purpose. But it could make you more, if you let it. I'd found it.

I don't know how long I was watching it rotate, as I climbed deeper and deeper into the tree. Mwinyi would later tell me that he'd been in the Star Chamber; they'd been eating and Okwu had been telling him a story about a Meduse meeting of chiefs long ago that had gone horribly wrong. "We knew you were off somewhere brooding," he said.

The ball was rotating faster and faster now with my current, humming with the trees. The hairs on my arms rose with the charge in the air. My *okuoko* slithered about me at my sides and back, old *otjize* still flaking from them to the floor. Then I was in space!

Infinite blackness.

Weightless. Flying.

Falling a bit.

Catching myself.

Then flying again.

I wanted to scream *and* laugh; I had become something more again. This time, I was so changed that I could fly through space without dying. I could live in open space. I moved through Saturn's ring of brittle metallic dust. It pelted our exoskeleton like chips of glittery ice. It felt pleasant, so I flew faster, resisting the urge to do barrel rolls because of Mwinyi and Okwu. New Fish was quiet, letting me take the lead. This was my mission. My purpose. And it was fantastic.

Living breath bloomed in me from the breathing room where I currently sat, the whirling golden ball humming with the trees. The metallic dust grew thick like a sandstorm and I stopped as some of it whirled before me in a way that reminded me of the golden ball.

"Who are you?" a voice asked. It spoke in the dialect of my family and it came from everywhere.

"Binti Ekeopara Zuzu Dambu Kaipka of Namib, that is my name," I blurted before I let myself think too hard about what was happening. "No," I said. "My name is Binti Ekeopara Zuzu Dambu Kaipka Meduse Enyi Zinariya New Fish of Namib." I waited a few moments and then decided to ask, "Who are you?"

"We are . . ." And for a moment, I heard nothing. Then the sound of their name split and split like a fractal in my mind. It was like the practice of treeing embodied in one word. Their name was an equation too complex, too various and varied to mentally fix into place, let alone put into a language that I was capable of uttering. It was beautiful and my joy in just letting it cartwheel and bounce about my mind was reflected in the color New Fish shined in the metallic storm of Saturn's ring.

When I could finally speak, I said, "You've called me here. Why? What is it you want?"

The rush of debris swirled before me into a funnel shape now.

"Did *we* call you here?" it asked, its voice almost playful.

"You did." I focused hard on the funnel, their name still in my mind vying for attention.

"That ball belongs to a people we've met. They only leave it to be found by those they feel should find them. They pack it between pieces of beautiful metal like a gift."

"What is it?" I asked.

"What do you think it is?"

I could see New Fish's light grow purpler with my annoyance. "You called me," I repeated. "Why?"

"Okay," it said. "We called you, yes. Through your zinariya object."

"I'm here now, finally. What do you want?"

There was a long pause. The dust swirled and swirled and for a moment, I was sure I saw a flash of red-orange light. I didn't bother wondering who these people were or where they had come from or what they even looked like. If

I was meant to find out, I would. If not, then I would not. If there was one thing I had learned in all my strange journeys it was that what would be would be and sometimes you wait to see. And this was fine, because at least I'd gotten to the bottom of the question of my *edan* and that odd vision and what was there was just as strange as I had imagined.

"Tell us about Oomza Uni," the voice said.

I was so shocked that I couldn't answer. Then I said, "What?"

"You are a student at Oomza Uni, no?"

"I am, but—"

"That is why we called on you. We want an opinion on the university that comes from someone like us."

"But . . . like you? How am I—"

"We're people of time and space. We move about experiencing, collecting, becoming more. This is the philosophy and culture of our equation. There's no one of our kind there, yet we hear it is the finest university in the galaxy. There is plenty we could learn from there and we'd like to apply. But first, we need a true recommendation of the place from someone we trust. We trust you."

"So you've known I would eventually be . . . what I now am, so you sent for me?"

"Yes. We are many things. What is your opinion of the university?"

"Well . . . I left my home to attend, nearly died on the way, and when I got there, it turned out to be the best experience I ever had as an academic. Excellent professors, excellent students, and excellent environment. It's the perfect place for me."

There was a pause and then it said, "Thank you."

And just like that, the dust and debris of Saturn was simply dust and debris again. A recommendation, that's all they needed. It was so . . . anticlimactic. Not that I was complaining.

For a few moments, I enjoyed the sensation of space and the flecks and larger chunks of stone bouncing off of New Fish's body. Then I had an idea and used one of New Fish's large pincers to catch two fist-sized stones tumbling about. As New Fish, I could "taste" the dust and stones and they had a tanginess that reminded me of the life salt scraped from the leaves of Undying trees and the sandstone from which I made my astrolabe. I stored them in one of New Fish's many outer crevices. When I returned to myself, the golden ball was on the floor, the trees were quiet, and Mwinyi was standing over me, a perplexed look on his face.

"What was that all about?" he asked.

"Not as much as I expected," I said with a laugh as I got to my feet.

Chapter 11

Ntu Ntu Bugs and Sunshine

New Fish landed in the yellow grassy field where I'd had my first Oomza Uni class—Treeing 101. The large field was between the Math, Weapons, and Organics Cities, and it was typically vacant. This day, there were a couple Meduse-like people with nets, probably catching ntu ntu bugs to study. The moment we landed, one of them roared and floated off, while the other puffed out gas and watched as a university shuttle glided up and waited for us to come out.

I said nothing as Mwinyi and Okwu moved down New Fish's walkway. In Okwu's excitement and Mwinyi's hesitation, they'd both forgotten. I was fine with this; I preferred to deal with the anxiety on my own. Well, as on my own as I could be now.

"*Walk slowly,*" New Fish said as I paused at the exit.

"I can't do anything else," I said, trying not to think about how naked I was. I had no *otjize* on my skin. The hot entrance into the atmosphere had been different this time because my connection to New Fish made me feel the discomfort of the heat. And the shift from New Fish's internally balanced gravity to that of Oomza Uni's still left me a bit weak and dizzy. The grass was so yellow that it practically glowed in the shine of Oomza Uni's two suns. I could smell the scent of the soil, grass, and the ntu ntu bugs who lived in the grass.

I heard Okwu speaking to someone further out and Mwinyi had taken his shoes off and bent down to touch the ground. His eyes were shut. I began to walk down the walkway. New Fish had said that I wouldn't be able to go far from her because I was technically a part of her now. However, she didn't know what "far" meant. Did this mean I couldn't leave the ship? That I couldn't go more than a few yards? We were about to find out. And what would happen if I went too far?

My feet touched the grass and I exhaled, looking back at the ship. I paused as I gazed upon her for the first time. She was bigger than the Root, but had the same natural grace. I smiled to myself. This was because both New Fish and the Root were alive. She wasn't shaped as much like a shrimp as her mother. She looked more like a water creature I couldn't name; she was bulbous in body that reminded me of the translucent Meduse ships. And here in the atmosphere and sunshine, her purple-pink flesh was detailed with thick lines of gold that rimmed the openings of fins and ran around both her sides. And she had eyes! How had I not known that she had enormous bright golden eyes? When I thought about looking through her eyes at Saturn, I could have sworn that I saw colors I couldn't name. So this made sense. Those glorious eyes looked at me now as I moved away from her, walking backward toward the Oomza shuttle and representatives who'd come to meet us.

"*You are alright?*" New Fish asked.

I nodded, grinning.

Slowly, I walked to the Oomza representatives, two crablike people, one with a rose-colored exoskeleton and the other green. Both of their bodies were wrapped in blue Oomza Uni cloth. Both had their astrolabes hanging from golden chains at the base of their left fore-claws and from their astrolabes came their cheerful voices.

"Welcome back, Binti," both proclaimed.

"Thank you," I said. "I hope our landing here wasn't too much of an issue. We didn't want everyone to make a big fuss at the launch port."

"It is what it is and we know you do what you do," the rose one said. "And your ship is small and living, so it's good for the grasses."

"President Haras says she can stay here for now," the green one said. "It would like to meet with you, Okwu, and the Mwinyi immediately."

"Just 'Mwinyi' is fine," he said, looking up from where he squatted with his hands to the soil.

"Mwinyi," the green one said. "We will drive you all. Your ship can rest, graze . . . does she need something else?"

I looked at New Fish. "Should I? Can I?" I asked.

"*I can fly with you.*"

And that's how we did it. With New Fish flying directly above. It was Oomza Uni, such a thing may not have been a common sight, but it probably wasn't bizarre here. Few things were.

Chapter 12

President Haras

The Oomza University president's name was something that sounded like the sound of the wind blowing over the desert sand dunes back home. To me, it sounded like "haaaaraaaaaaaasssssss," so I called it Haras. It didn't mind, as long as I prefaced it with the title of "President." I'd first met President Haras at the meeting directly upon leaving the Third Fish, when I pled the case of the Meduse and their violent killing of all but one of the Khoush people on board.

My first impression was that it looked like one of the gods of the Enyi Zinariya (well, back then I'd thought, "Desert People"). President Haras was a spiderlike person who was about the width of Okwu and as tall as me. And like its name, it seemed to be made of wind, gray and undulating here and not quite there. I'd met with it several times over my year at Oomza Uni and I loved its office.

Positioned in the administrative building in Central City, President Haras's office sat at the top of the hivelike sandstone building. Nothing but a great bubble of blue-tinted crystal, the floor was a soft red grass that warmed with the sun. Embedded in the wall opposite the triangular door was President Haras's astrolabe, which liked to buzz whenever anyone walked up to the entrance.

"Take your sandals off," I said to Mwinyi.

He quickly did so, looking around with awe at the blue dome. He was grinning again, something he'd been doing since we'd landed on Oomza Uni. He laughed to himself with glee when he set foot on the soft grass of President Haras's office. "I can hear them here, too," he said. He giggled.

"What is wrong with Mwinyi?" Okwu asked me in Meduse, as we walked toward President Haras.

"He can talk to living things," I said. "And do something called 'deep grounding.' Plus, he's never been on a different planet."

"Will his happiness kill him?" Okwu asked.

"President Haras," I said, ignoring both Okwu and Mwinyi, who was still giggling, and looked at the grass.

"Welcome back, Binti and Okwu," it said in Otjihimba. It stood in the center of the dome and for a moment, it completely disappeared and then it was back. I was used to this, but Mwinyi was not and behind me, I heard him gasp. "Just in time for some rest and then the start of the next academic cycle. You will be staying for that?"

"Yes," Okwu and I said.

"Good," it said. "And my *greatest* welcome is to you, Mwinyi Njem of the Enyi Zinariya."

"I am so happy to be here, President Haras," Mwinyi said.

"You are also the first of your people to be here," President Haras said. "The Zinariya have written research papers about your ancestors and speculated about your people in current times. From what I understand, a group of Zinariya students wants to reconnect with your people. It's been a long time."

When Mwinyi only stared at President Haras with his mouth hanging open, President Haras chuckled. "You are a harmonizer?"

"Yes, Mma," he said. Then he frowned. "I'm sorry. I don't know if . . . do I call you Oga? President? In my village, we have only men and women and some who are both, neither, or more, but all human. At least, since the Zinariya left us long ago."

"What do you call Okwu?"

"I just go with what Binti says," he said. "But in my head, I often call it 'he.' "

Beside me, Okwu puffed out a burst of gas and I looked at my feet smiling.

Mwinyi looked at me and then Okwu, then shrugged.

"You may call me 'Mma,' if you like," President Haras said.

Mwinyi nodded. "Thank you, Mma."

"So," President Haras said, turning and scuttling toward the far side of the dome. The three of us followed. President Haras always liked to walk in circles around the dome as it spoke. It looked up through the top of the high ceiling at New Fish, who hovered just above the building. "Things didn't go as expected?"

We told it everything, me talking sometimes, other times Okwu and Mwinyi. President Haras clicked its forelegs and a few times seemed to completely disappear as it listened, but was mostly quiet and fully present physically. I couldn't help crying when I talked about when the Root was burned and I was sure my family was dead. Mwinyi told President Haras about what he'd seen from afar when I stabbed the owl-like creature's feather into my flesh to activate the zinariya. He'd said it was like something had erupted. "The ground shook enough for small cracks to open up around me and from where the Ariya's cavern was, or at least near it. And there was a blast of blue-purple light," he said. "But it rose and fell like water."

When I'd come back to myself, the Ariya's clothes had been on fire and I'd been horrified that I'd somehow called up current and lost control of it. What Mwinyi described was even stranger. When Okwu told of its killing of all those Khoush soldiers as my home burned with my family inside it, I felt a rush of hot fury and pleasure. My parents had not died, but the Root, a place dearer to Osemba Himbas than even the Osemba House, had been burned down out of Khoush spite. The Khoush did *not* get to walk away free from that. I knew my glee at hearing about the justified killing was part of my Meduse side and it bothered me . . . but not as much as it would have a few weeks ago. I let myself feel it.

As we told it all, we walked and walked the circle of the president's office. Only as I told of my death and New Fish's resurrection of me did President Haras stop walking to ask questions.

"But they agreed on the truce," it said. "Why did they start warring?"

"I don't know," I said. "Someone shot at the Meduse chief and then everything just exploded."

"The Khoush are a terrible people," Okwu said.

I frowned, looking at it. "The Meduse killed my friends in cold blood," I said. "A ship full of unarmed students and professors who'd have been happy to talk things through and help get the stinger back. How different are the Meduse?"

"We acted out of duty, loyalty, and honor, Binti," Okwu said.

I was shaking now, the tips of my *okuoko* quivering and against my back. I was seeing Heru again, his chest exploding. And not for the first time, I wondered if that stinger had been Okwu's stinger. It could have been. At the time, I did not know Okwu very well. My memory could not identify it among the many Meduse committing *moojh-ha kibira* right before my eyes. Even when I was later stung in the Meduse ship, Okwu had been beside the chief, but I'd seen Okwu move very fast, it could have zipped behind me in that moment.

"Binti," President Haras said, putting a foreleg on my

shoulder. I flinched and it pressed its foreleg to me harder. "Look at the grass. Remember what we say?"

"It grows because it's alive," I whispered, looking at the red grass. "It grows because it's alive." This was a mantra President Haras had taught me to say whenever I was in its office and a panic attack descended on me. The grass I stood on with my bare feet was a deep red like blood, but it wasn't bleeding, it was alive. *Red was not always bad,* I repeated to myself. *I wore red, the Himba wore it,* otjize *is red. When I speak through the zinariya, my words are red.* "It grows because it's alive." I inhaled, exhaled, and felt better. Calmer. However, I didn't look at Okwu.

"Mwinyi," President Haras said. "Do you remember what happened?"

"At this point, I was at the base of the Root," he said. "I'd heard . . . I'm . . . the lightning may have allowed me to hear it without touching . . . I'm a harmonizer, I—"

"Yes, I understand what you can do," President Haras said. "You can communicate with and to living things without necessarily knowing their language. You're a different type of harmonizer than Binti."

Mwinyi looked relieved and nodded. "It's hard to explain to people."

"You're at Oomza Uni, not many surprises here," it said.

"I also, my feet. I can ground, now. Maybe seeing Binti die triggered it."

"That's most likely," Haras said. "Those who bond closely with planets often develop grounding tendencies.

You're a born harmonizer and natural worlds appeal to you; it's surprising you haven't been grounding since birth. So you heard something?"

"Yes, I was listening to the Root, realizing that it *was* a root, no, a tree, an Undying tree. Just growing underground, upside down. Binti had spoken and it seemed everything was great. We'd won. I did look up just in time to see the chief shot. But I also saw the Khoush president's face. He didn't look like he knew that was coming. And then he looked a little angry. But I saw his general Kuw, too. *He* looked ready. He ran at Binti."

I blinked, remembering. General Kuw had grabbed me. I'd punched him. Twice. Then Okwu had fought with him, but there was shooting and Okwu had had to shield itself. Kuw had still gotten away. And I had been killed.

"I think there was disagreement among the Khoush," Mwinyi was saying. "I think someone knew."

"Maybe," President Haras said. "Maybe the Khoush president's second or third in command betrayed him like the Himba Council betrayed Binti. Or maybe someone's weapon was too sensitive. Or maybe one small soldier didn't like what she or he was seeing and decided to change everything. We may never know." It looked up at New Fish. "You are not the first Oomza Uni student to be paired with a ship, Binti."

I looked up from the grass to stare at the president.

It crossed its forelegs, shook them, and faded a bit, laughter. "Again, I remind you all that you're at Oomza

Uni. There are few surprises here. Most things have been researched, documented, and obsessed over. You will find entire dissertations written about paired people, especially ships and those who travel within them because such pairs tend to be the most traveled and knowledgeable of people. There are paired professors at Oomza Uni." It paused and then said, "We're done here for today. Binti, you'll go to the New Alien Medical Building. It's near here. I've scheduled you to be examined. They'll be able to tell you how far you can go from your New Fish. If you'd like to speak with paired people, just ask."

I frowned. I didn't really want anyone looking too closely at my blood or my body, me. I knew this was Oomza Uni and they had probably seen people like me before, but I wasn't sure I wanted to know the details.

"Mwinyi, would you be interested in testing to get into the university? You're of human age and you'd be the first of your kind here. Plus, it seems you're a master harmonizer, gifted in your own right."

"No," Mwinyi said. He looked at his bare feet and shook his head. "I'm sorry, Mma. That was rude. No, Mma, President Haras. I'm here for Binti . . . and Okwu. I don't want to be a student. I learn best by wandering, really."

President Haras gazed at him for several moments with its many black eyes and then said, "Well, as an honored guest at Oomza Uni, you're free to sit in on whatever classes you like. Maybe you'll eventually change your mind."

Mwinyi smiled and said, "Thank you," though his tone clearly said he would not.

"I'll have to meet with the committee about the Meduse-Khoush War," President Haras said. "It's not our fight, but we are involved. The Khoush Oomza Uni students harbored the stinger that restarted it and Oomza Uni endorsed the new pact and Okwu's visit. We'll meet and discuss, then we will act. If we need you, we will call. But until then, don't worry too much. This fight is old and if the Enyi Zinariya are going to help the Himba, then at least your families will be safe. With you gone, the Khoush will not bother with the Himba, I don't think."

What about when I go back? I wondered.

"Have you reached out to your father?" the president asked.

"I will," was all I said, looking away. *Do they really need to know I'm alive yet? After all that? With what is probably happening over there right now?* I preferred to allow my family to focus on the present, for the time being. And that present meant getting away from the Meduse-Khoush War and opening themselves to the Enyi Zinariya. I felt a pang of guilt for not being there and then quickly pushed it away.

"Ah yes, and we've already heard from the people you met in Saturn's ring," President Haras said. "They've been tested and, oh my, those people have several youths and even a few elders who will make fine students here."

"Really? Already?"

"Oh yes," President Haras said. "They don't waste time when they are sure of something. And they said the recommendation they got made them very, very sure. I suspect at some point one of you three will meet them."

I glanced at Mwinyi. He was grinning again.

Chapter 13

Medical

Twenty-five hours later, I walked up the path to the white building. On the front was a symbol that was a combination of individuals (only one humanoid) standing together. Leaving my dorm room, ignoring the stares of classmates, and feeling the sun directly on my skin and *okuoko,* had been extremely difficult. Not only had most people heard bits and pieces of what had happened to me on Earth after a few students overheard a professor who'd just spoken with the president, but I *looked* very different. Without my *otjize,* my dark brown skin was that much more noticeable, compared to the few other human students who were all Khoush. In addition, without the *otjize* covering them, my ten thick *okuoko* were on full display. I was a human with soft transparent blue tentacles with darker blue dots at their tips that hung nearly to my knees now. People associated me even more with Okwu, whom they feared so much already.

My friend Haifa was the only one who'd come to my room and demanded I tell her every detail. And as I had, she'd stared and stared at my face and I'd felt so uncomfortable that I'd begun to sweat and had to tree a little in order to finish. I'd missed Haifa and even in my discomfort, I was happy to see her. However, her staring and the feeling of being naked left me tired.

Now at my medical exam, I felt the same anxious fatigue. I'd considered bringing Mwinyi, but he seemed to be having too much fun running around barefoot and meeting everyone for me to drag him along. Okwu had disappeared into its dorm, telling me nothing but, "Go to your exam. I will be here." As I walked into the building, New Fish hovered above.

~

My doctor was surprisingly a human being, a tall plump Khoush woman who was about my mother's age. She wore flowing black robes and a sparkling earring on each ear that matched her equally green eyes. President Haras probably had made this happen. She towered over me as she held out a hand. "Hello, Binti. My name is Tuka."

I shook her hand and said, "Hello" as I glanced around the small room. It looked similar to the patient rooms back home, though the examination table was much wider, longer, and sturdier than any I'd seen.

"I spoke at length with President Haras this morning," she said. She smiled, looking keenly at my *okuoko*. "You're amazing, my dear."

"Thank you," I said quietly.

"I want to put you through a series of tests—blood, skin, digestive, brain; I want to look at everything. We'll be able to talk about the results in a few hours."

"Hours?" I said.

She nodded. "And yes, I'll be able to tell you how far you and your ship can go from each other."

My heart started racing and I sat down heavily on the yellow chair behind me.

"What's the matter?" she asked, worried.

"I'm afraid of what you'll find."

"We'll definitely find some interesting things, but nothing you can't deal with, Binti. You already are what you are and you're fine."

"Am I?" I asked.

She patted me on the shoulder. "Let's get started. You can stay sitting. We'll test your reflexes."

~

Afterward, I was in the waiting room for three hours, too paralyzed with worry to get up and move when a Meduse-like person came and hovered beside me. It was probably worried too, because it puffed out gas constantly and barely bothered to suck it back in. I would have had my astrolabe play some soft music for me, but mine was broken and, unlike my *edan,* its broken remains weren't anywhere to be found when I'd awoken on New Fish. Since I'd died and returned, I'd been able to speak through the zinariya with ease, no more vertigo and no gaping tunnel or strange planet appeared behind me anymore. However, speaking to my grandmother or Mwinyi through the zinariya was out of the question because they'd both just ask me if I'd gotten the test results yet. At some point, I curled up on the blue chair and fell asleep.

I immediately awoke when my name was called and followed the small hovering droid back to the same patient room I'd been in before with Dr. Tuka. She sat on a high chair with a tray on which she had her astrolabe projecting a chart before her eyes.

"Have a seat," she said without looking away from it.

I sat in the yellow chair, unable to hide my shivering.

"So, your tests have all come back," she said, turning to me.

"Please, tell me how far I can go first," I blurted.

"About five miles on land and she can fly about seven miles up," she said. "That's not so bad, is it?"

I smiled and said, "No. Thank the Seven."

"But unless she follows, no more taking university and solar shuttles, okay? New Fish can take you."

I nodded and then asked the question I'd been dreading most, "What happens if we get too far from each other? Will . . . we die?"

"*She* won't," Dr. Tuka said. "But *you* might, if the distance happens very fast and is a lot. But first, there will be terrible pain. It's different for everyone. Just don't do it."

She paused, waiting for me to ask anything else. I didn't want to know anything else.

"Okay, so your DNA is very interesting, Binti," she said. "You're . . .

"Am I . . . am I still human?" I asked.

"Do you think you are?"

"I mean, well, that's not . . ."

"You are a Himba girl, right? That's what you say you are?"

"Yes, but . . ." I touched my *okuoko* and smiled sheepishly. "Aren't I equally New Fish microbes? Isn't that why I'm alive?"

"Your DNA is Himba, Enyi Zinariya, and Meduse . . . and some, but not much, New Fish," she said. "But your microbes are mostly from New Fish, yes. Your microbes exist with your cells, so this blend is what makes you, you. So you are different from what you were born as, certainly. But as I said before, you're healthy."

I breathed a sigh of relief.

"There's more, however," Dr. Tuka said. "Something you should know."

I frowned. "Like what?"

"Well, at this point, this may not be much of a surprise or issue since you've already spent a year at Oomza Uni, met many people, and so on." She paused and looked at the virtual chart. Then she said, "You're seventeen Earth years old, correct?"

I nodded, but she wasn't even looking at me.

"Have you ever thought about having children?"

I frowned more deeply. "Of course," I said. "For me to do all that I've done and never have children, what kind of Himba—"

She turned to me. The look on her face made me close my mouth.

"What if Okwu gave birth to it?" she said.

"What?!"

"This will happen. Not now, but in time."

"But—"

"And if you were to have a baby, it would have your *okuoko* because Meduse DNA is strong. It bullies its way into all offspring."

"But Okwu and I aren't—" I paused, thinking of who Okwu was to me and then I thought about when I'd kissed Mwinyi.

"On top of this, if you were to have a child, you would pass New Fish microbes to it and there is the possibility that your child would be part New Fish as well. Though no likelihood of the link. Also—"

"Stop!" I screeched, my eyes closed. "Enough. Enough!" There was a ringing in my ears and it was getting louder. My face was growing hot and felt as if something were squeezing my head. I was both falling and rising. "Even my astrolabe broke," I breathed. "The chip is corrupted. I have no documented identity." I giggled wildly and screamed, "What *am* I? I'm so much," with tears welling in my eyes.

"I . . . I didn't go on my pilgrimage when I went home. That was supposed to complete me as a woman in my village. Instead, my mere *presence* started a *war*! In my home! *They burned my home!* And they killed me! I died! And then I came back as . . . am I really even me?" I was on my feet now. Pacing the small room. Smacking my forehead.

On the room's counter was a vase full of soft-looking yellow flowers with petals that each looked like bladders of water. I grabbed one and crushed the flower in my fist as I stared at Dr. Tuka, who calmly watched me. The liquid that burst from each petal dribbled down my wrist to my elbow and the room suddenly smelled sweet and earthy. "My past and present have become more and *now my future*?"

I sobbed, throwing the crushed flower to my feet and sinking to the floor. I rested my head in my hands. "I have always liked myself, Dr. Tuka." I looked up at her. "I *like* who I am. I *love* my family. I wasn't running away from home. I don't *want* to change, to grow! Nothing . . . everything . . . I don't want all this . . . this weirdness! It's too heavy! I just want to *be*."

Dr. Tuka watched me, quiet.

"Am I human?" I asked. As I desperately stared at her, as she said nothing, she grew blurry as my eyes teared up more. For the first time since I'd left home, I wondered if I should have left home.

"Binti," Dr. Tuka said. "In your tribe a woman marries a man, and in doing so, marries his family, correct?"

"Yes," I whispered.

"She marries a man chosen by her family and herself, who will provide for and protect her and nourish her being."

"Yes."

"This is the path to respect among the Himba. I read up on them before seeing you. So see it this way: You're paired with New Fish and Okwu, each of whom has a family. Your family is bigger than any Himba girl's ever was. And twice, you were supposed to die. And here you stand healthy and strong . . ." She chuckled and then added, "And strange. There is no person like you at this school."

I sat down again, still shaking from all the information, all the reality. "I'm sorry I did that to your flower," I said. "I don't . . . I don't normally destroy things."

"It will grow another one," she said.

I nodded. "Good."

"Go and study, Binti," Dr. Tuka said, turning back to her virtual chart. "I'm also scheduling an appointment for you with your therapist."

~

The moment I told New Fish that we could be apart for five miles on land and seven in the air, New Fish took off, gleefully zooming up about two miles, then free-falling back to land and zooming large circles around the area. Still, she couldn't return to the field that she'd liked so much because it was over a hundred miles away. Not without me. And I wanted to return to my dorm and lie down. I'd been so worried and now things were sort of okay. I was okay. Sort of.

There was a small open field near my dorm. It didn't have the tasty yellow grass or the ntu ntu bugs New Fish wanted to taste, and students liked to walk through it on the way to class. But it was relatively quiet and two other living ships stayed there. New Fish approved.

~

I closed the door behind me and sank to the floor. Then I quickly got up. I needed to check on the fresh jar of *otjize* I'd mixed last night. I took the lid off, sniffed it, and looked at the red-orange paste. It still looked thin. Maybe another day. Another day of being naked. I sighed, putting it back on the windowsill where the light from Oomza Uni's large moon and tomorrow's sunshine would heat it. I'd just lain on my bed for a nap when there was a knock on my door. Groaning, I reached into my pocket to grab my astrolabe so I could see who it was. Then I remembered that my astrolabe was back on Earth. Broken, probably left in the dirt when I'd been shot.

"Who's there?" I said.

"Open the door," Haifa said.

I smiled and said, "Open."

Haifa stood there grinning at me and behind her stood Mwinyi, who wasn't grinning at all. "Saw him in the lobby and assumed he was coming up here. I decided to show him the way."

"I've been here twice already," Mwinyi said, cracking a small smile.

"Okay, I just wanted to walk with you," she said, batting her eyes flirtatiously at him. "You seemed lonely." From the moment Haifa had set eyes on Mwinyi, she'd been in "love."

Mwinyi laughed. "I appreciate the company," he said, sitting in the wooden chair at my study desk.

Haifa giggled and sat on the bed with me.

"You didn't tell me you were back," Mwinyi said.

"I assumed you were busy with all your new friends," I said with a smirk. "When you had time, you'd come here."

Where I'd had a hard time making friends since coming to Oomza Uni because people were afraid of Okwu, Mwinyi was a friend magnet. From the moment the university gave him a room in the mostly humanoid dorm beside mine yesterday, despite the fact that he refused to become an Oomza Uni student, he'd been incredibly popular. I was there with him when he entered the dorm. He'd immediately struck up a conversation with the dorm's elder, a treelike individual who spoke in a series of cracking and creaking sounds. Somehow, Mwinyi was able to understand it. I watched him relax and give that intense look and then start to make gestures. This dorm elder liked Mwinyi so much that after introducing Mwinyi to practically everyone on his floor, it and several others stayed in

Mwinyi's room to help him set up and just to "talk." I'd ended up quietly saying goodbye and heading to my dorm. From the start, I saw that people of all kinds were simply attracted to him.

"What'd they tell you?" he asked.

Haifa looked at me and yet again, I felt my nakedness. I glanced at my jar of still-stewing *otjize* and wanted to groan. One more day. Hopefully.

"Stop looking at me like that," I muttered.

Haifa laughed. "I'm just glad you're back," she said. "Even the Bear said she missed you."

"No she didn't," I said, rolling my eyes. "The Bear doesn't like anyone."

The Bear lived in one of the rooms down the hall. She was mostly bushy brown hair. The Bear and I never spoke much, but we'd often found ourselves sitting side by side on one of the large couches in the main room. I'd always liked her because I imagined she understood one's need to be covered.

"I talk to the Bear all the time," Haifa said. "She asked why you'd left for break instead of staying with all of us. She wondered if you didn't like us."

"Binti, what'd they say?" Mwinyi insisted.

"I'm okay, Mwinyi," I said. "I can move five miles from New Fish on land and she can fly about seven miles high."

Before I even finished saying this, Mwinyi slumped in his chair with relief. I laughed. He stood up suddenly and then seemed unsure of what to do next, as he looked at

Haifa and me on the bed. Haifa looked from me to Mwinyi and back to me. Her eyebrows rose. "Oh!" she said. She looked at me and pointed at Mwinyi. I nodded.

"You could have told me," she said, smirking.

"I just got back yesterday. There's a lot I have to tell you."

Haifa got up.

"Tomorrow . . . do you and the Bear want to come with me to see the Falls?" I asked her. I turned to Mwinyi, "You too, and Okwu. I've been meaning to see them since I came here but never had the time." I didn't say the rest of what I was thinking, which was, *Better see them while I can. You never know tomorrow.*

Haifa kissed me on the cheek. "Of course. It'll be a good homecoming thing for us. I know the Bear will. She loves the Falls with all those colors."

"Mwinyi?" I asked.

He nodded.

"I hope you all don't mind that we'll have to fly there in New Fish instead of taking the shuttle."

Haifa beamed and clapped her hands. "Yes! Everyone will be so jealous. You do know that everyone in this dorm has wanted a ride on your ship since you got here, right?"

"Really?" I asked.

"Yes," Mwinyi and Haifa both said. Then they laughed.

When the door shut behind Haifa, Mwinyi turned to me. "What else did they tell you?"

"I don't really want to talk about it right now, okay?" I said.

He came across the room to me. I looked down, trying to avoid his eyes. He took my chin and lifted my face. "Are you alright?" he asked. As I looked into his eyes, I felt all my defenses relax. Looking into his eyes was like being a mirror who was looking into another mirror. Universes.

"Everything is going to be fine," I said.

"Everything is going to be fine," he repeated.

He stepped closer, paused, then closer. He took me in his arms and slowly I relaxed and then finally lay my head on his shoulder, turning my head to his bushy hair. Somehow, he still smelled like the desert. I kissed him on the neck and soon found my way to his lips.

We forgot ourselves for a while.

Chapter 14

Shape Shifter

In the morning, I sat at the windowsill with my jar of *otjize* in my lap.

The first sun had just risen, shining its lush yellow light into my room. I tilted my damp face toward it, enjoying the warmth as I leaned against the wall. My *okuoko* were wet from the long shower I'd taken, but they dried quickly in the morning light. The transparent blue flesh that they were remained soft once dry, it never grew chapped like my skin when I didn't apply *otjize*. I opened my eyes and they fell on the two large stones I'd had New Fish pluck from Saturn's ring.

After digging them out of the crevice I'd had New Fish hide them in, letting the ice encasing parts of them melt off, I'd brought the stones to my room and spent several minutes examining them. I'd tasted them and indeed they had the same tang as the salt from Undying trees and god stone. Then I decided to test for what I suspected by tree-ing and called up a complex current. Splitting the current into a treelike shape, I laid it over each stone and watched how the network of current sank through it with control and ease. I smiled widely. Not only would I use these stones to carve out each intricate dial, womb, rete, star pointer, plate, and circuit board, but the astrolabe I would build would be like no astrolabe any Himba has ever made.

I picked up the jar and held it between my palms. It was also warm, as if it had absorbed the sun. I put on my favorite red wrapper and matching top, one of the outfits I'd brought with me when I'd first arrived on Oomza Uni. The material was soft and worn from many washings and wind faded because I'd gone off into the desert many times wearing this very outfit.

The night of my return, I'd gone to the usual spot in the nearby forest to collect the clay. I'd dug a small hole and marked it with twigs and, apparently, while I was away one of the round-bodied beasts I'd seen a couple times had made the place its rest spot. The top layer of clay was coated with rough black hairs and pressed with hooved footprints. I scraped off this layer and dug out a large clump of the clay. I mixed it with the special black flower oil I still had in my room and then I started counting down.

Now I whispered, "Zero," and twisted the jar open. The smell that wafted out made me grin. I looked at the Night Masquerade costume I'd hung on the wall beside the window and said to it, "Yes. It's ready." I dug my right index and middle fingers into it, my two fingers I'd had since I was born. Then I smeared it on my left hand, thinking hard about the fact that this was the first time it had ever had *otjize* on it. It went on smooth, like something that belonged there. Then I fell into my routine. I always ended with my face.

With a sigh, I dug out a large dollop and massaged it into my cheeks. For the first time in a while, I felt like myself. When I was done applying it to my skin, I started rolling it on my ten *okuoko,* hiding the clear blue with speckles at the tips. Because they were so long, they required quite a bit of *otjize.* As I started rolling the last one between my palms, I heard the sound of metal clinking and then a soft hum from behind me.

Slowly, I turned around. There on my desk, the golden ball and its triangle metal slivers were rising and hovering about five inches in the air. As I watched, the pieces were drawn to the rotating golden ball. They clinked some more as they reattached themselves, trying one shape and then shifting to another. Stellated, square, star, cylinder. I crept over to it, my hand still clutching my last *otjize*-free *okuoko.*

I quickly climbed the tree, grasping at the Pythagorean theorem. I called up a current as I brought my face about a foot from it. The moment I held up my hands, the current softly buzzing between them, the pieces suddenly decided to stick. I actually *felt* the force the golden ball made in order to pull the metal pieces to it. Then the object fell to my desk with a *thunk.*

"What?" I asked, touching the tip of the shiny silver pyramid it had become.

When it did nothing else, I went back to my jar of *otjize* and finished doing my hair. I rubbed a bit more into the five anklets I now wore on each ankle, took a last look at my new *edan,* and then left to meet up with Mwinyi, Okwu, Haifa, and the Bear. When school started back up in a few Earth days, I'd have something interesting to show Professor Okpala. However, for the time being all I cared about was finally seeing the Falls with my friends.

And when we got there, it really was like witnessing a beautiful dream.

Acknowledgments

Three Augusts in a row, Binti's story came to me. It happened each time I returned to Buffalo, New York, after spending the summer with my family in the south Chicago suburbs of Illinois. In the August of 2016, I wanted to take a break from writing. I didn't think I'd have the ending to Binti's story for a while, years even, and I was fine with that. Then I sat down one evening and the entire story came to me. First the end, then the middle, then the beginning.

Over three days, I scribbled down the plot in the little Ankara cloth-covered journal I'd bought in the Lagos airport. But I didn't answer the call to adventure immediately. I had courses to teach and another novel to edit. I went to South Africa and gazed at the Lion's Head, went to the Arizona desert and followed a Pepsis wasp, I saw the White House while it was still worth seeing, and I had a conversation about microbes with a Ph.D. student during a lunch with the African Cultural Association at the University of Illinois, Urbana-Champaign. When winter break arrived, the moment I took off my professor hat to give the writer's cap that I always wear some fresh air, whatever it is that takes hold of me to make me write descended on me.

So first and foremost I want to thank that thing that

grabs, that whispers, that urgently tells. I'd like to thank my Ancestors, who walk in front of, behind, beside, fly above, and swim beneath me. Thanks to my daughter, Anyaugo, for demanding to know what happened to Okwu. Thanks to my editor Lee Harris and my agent, Don Maass, for their excellent feedback. And thanks to my beta reader Angel Maynard, who responded with, "Mind blown!" after reading the first clean draft. And finally, thank you to the rest of my immediate family, my mother, sisters Ifeoma and Ngozi, brother Emezie, nephews Dika and Chinedu, and niece Obioma. Without you all energizing my life, the Binti Trilogy would never ever have happened. I love you all.